I0529688

SWEET SCORPION
By Ami

M.O.R.E. Publishers
St. Louis, MO

SWEET SCORPION
By Ami

Ghost Writer – Carolyn Ferrante-Crymes
Cover Design – Edwin Marcellus T. Grider
Inside Cover Design – Timothy Ferrante

Printed in the United States of America

ISBN 978-0-9801647-8-7

M.O.R.E. Publishers Corp.
P.O. Box 38285
St. Louis, MO 63138

Angelee Coleman Grider, Editor

SWEET SCORPION

Dedication

This book is dedicated to my children, my parents, my siblings, and to the end of homelessness, hunger, illness, drug addiction, and economic oppression.

Table of Contents

Chapter 1:
INTRODUCTION

I got married at the age of 18, after dating Charles for only two years. In fact, he proposed to me only after dating me for two months and 15 days. At 16, I thought the proposal was only a "game" and a prelude to another intimate question. Besides, my mind was still on my high school sweetheart with whom I still shared a locker. Even though we had broken up; it happened in the middle of the school year and there were no empty lockers available. That made it hard for my mind to be on this new guy.

Bob, and I were still together everyday even though the romantic/puppy love part of the relationship had ended. We just broke up and started relationships with other people. As I think about it now I have to admit that we were both just being too stubborn and egomaniacal to get back together.

Charles, on-the-other-hand, definitely had impeccable qualities. He had a good job at a somewhat prestigious company, so he told me. He also said he had graduated from our rival high school, which made things more intriguing. He drove a rather nice-looking, almost new car. Mostly, he pursued me to the point of getting on my nerves (if I had any at that age.) Of course I did not check any of the information to see if anything he said was true. I was just fascinated with what I heard. Besides, my pride would not allow me to go begging my "ex" to come back (which was his stipulation for a reconciliation, according to his friends). I had quit him too many times before because of his infidelity.

Also, Bob was three years my senior, and I was not ready for what he needed in a relationship. So logically, why not go with a guy who declared his undying love for me? Charles' devoted behavior was annoying, yet consistently sincere. Plus, Charles also "claimed" that he had no girlfriends and no children.

"OK", I'm thinking, "this will be a painless, stress-free relationship."

In the meantime, my "ex" and I are at school everyday trying to establish a 'we're just friends' relationship - forget the love, and get use to being with other people. The new life began on May 21st, my 17th birthday.

I arrived home from school and there was a huge, full sheet-cake on the table. In those days a full sheet-cake was over a yard long and nearly as wide. Getting this for a present was strange since I had no birthday party planned for me; nor did my parents. My parents just said that the "new guy dropped it off on his way to work as a birthday present". Then my parents gave me the card that he left with the cake. In my mind I was thinking, "What am I going to do with all this cake? This is the dumbest gift in the world". Strangely enough for some reason though, the gift touched my heart. Since my sister's birthday was 2 days later, my mom took the cake to the nursery school and had a birthday party for my sister and the 3 year olds there.

Charles was really a nice, sweet person. I started to pay a little more attention to him after that; and I began appreciating the person who had been chasing/pursuing me. He was just the opposite of the other person who was "someone who I knew loved me, but flirted with other girls behind my back and sometimes bodaciously, in front of my face. The cheating was my "frigid fault", according to Bob's friends. I was only 15 & 16. I was supposed to be very firm about being frigid.

Oh, well, a few months later, in August, Charles proposed to me twice. He said that he was willing to wait until I was ready for intimacy, but he thought that rushing into marriage would solve that problem. My family had planned for me to go to college, since I had been the family's bookworm, before I transferred to public school. There in public school, I was environmental culture shock. After being in private school for nine years, the public school mainstream was truly an extreme adjustment. Trying to study for the MCAT or anything related to med school was a pipe dream and out of the question. Still, I told Charles that the only way I would marry him would be if he agreed to let me go to college. We had agreed that neither he nor I wanted any children. They would hinder my college efforts anyway. So he agreed on college and we agreed on no babies.

Then I decided to tell my parents about the proposal. Of course my parents were devastated. They both literally went out on the porch and just stared into the sky. I didn't know what they were asking the gods up there, but I could imagine a few things, because they came back in and asked me if I were pregnant or something. They did not know that Charles was from a family that married very young (some at the age of 14 yrs. old), and he had been taught that marriage was a way to make a girl feel secure in her relationship. Marriage supposedly would help her trust, and hopefully love him.

"NO!" I defended. "I am not pregnant".

Besides, I always felt that having too many children before I bought my dream home would prevent me from ever getting that dream home. Plus, I came from a private school run by nuns and I came from a family that would have found a way to hide a teenage pregnancy, after they had a conniption. Well, my father was relieved to hear that I was not pregnant, but said, "If Charles wanted to marry you, he'd better be man enough to ask me himself." My father did not think Charles should have sent me to break the news. So Charles made an appointment to see my dad at our house.

Of course when he arrived, my brothers were sitting outside on the front porch with me. They started laughing and teasing him for being crazy enough to talk to "my" dad. I even remember that when my older sister was dating, my dad would send guys home that didn't dress properly enough to visit his daughter. Jeans were "out" in those days. The droopy drawers' guys of today would probably have gotten stoned or shot at my dad's house.

Well after talking to Charles, my dad finally said that he would give us his blessing. He would give the blessing though, only if we would wait until I graduated from high school, which was in about ten months. Charles agreed and then took me to look at wedding rings. We put the set I chose in the layaway. He also had my name tattooed on his arm as a surprise gesture of his love for me.

After Labor Day, school began along with the beginning of our engagement. Routinely, first period was always homeroom and for the seniors, homeroom was in the auditorium. We were seated by sections in alphabetical order. I was relieved that my first boyfriend and I would get new lockers this year! However, his last name began with 'Ba' and mine began with 'Bu'. Yes, we were in the same section. The Ba's were a couple of rows before the Bu's.

After we were all seated and the announcements were made, everyone in the rows in front of me started turning around in their seats looking at me. At first I turned around to look behind me to see at what everyone was looking. When I turned back around, I noticed that the person who had started everyone staring my way was my ex. He had turned around in his seat and was staring at me in a dreamy-eyed manner. It was written all over his face that he was truly missing me. He looked as if he was wondering how we would get through our last year without each other.

I hesitantly thought back to the time when I had gone to the local recreation center one evening to see him box. He was a well-known boxer at the school and in the neighborhood. The coaches said that my "ex" was so good that he beat one of the Spinks in their younger days. I remember that when Bob stepped into the ring, he hushed the crowd, turned to me and blew me a kiss, then commenced to knocking his opponent out, technically. He was very dramatic and romantic. Whimsically, he was really the class comic and was voted to be recognized for that. He had been also voted for being "most athletic" and "most popular". The advisors would only let him choose one title, so he chose "most popular". He did anything for attention and/or a laugh.

Then situations changed. I remembered a time when I would call him and his family mysteriously started asking me what was my last name. They had never done that before, so it was more than a woman's intuition that he must have been seeing another girl with the same first name as mine. So after a week or two of inquisitions, a guy at school was tired of me being fooled behind my back. He told me when and where Bob met the other girl - under some steps every morning before school started.

He said, "If you want to catch him, to see for yourself, be there at that time."

I caught Bob with a girl that I knew! She did have the same 1st name as mine. Later that day, after I caught them together, he brought her to me because she wanted to apologize. Then, he left notes all over the school stating that he was apologizing to me. He got everybody involved in persuading me to accept his apology. The gesture was so dramatically romantic. I finally accepted it and we were back together as if nothing had happened. That was definitely love!

Whoa, now back from my day dreaming. I had to remember that I was engaged to be married, and Bob's first child with his new girlfriend, was conceived almost immediately after we broke up. So we began senior year with Bob now being a father to a newborn. Unbelievably, the mother of the child had transferred to our school. She was a junior, so she was not in the auditorium. Thank goodness! It didn't matter though; I never strayed away from my own engagement nor disrespected her. We all survived the last year. Bob and his baby's mama broke up anyway, for other reasons though, not because of me.

I got married and Bob even came to my wedding. Charles said that it was okay to invite him. They had shook hands when Charles picked me up at school one day. Bob had walked up and introduced himself in order to stop everybody from trying to promote a boxing match between the two. The rumor was that students were really discussing placing bets on who would win. I was proud of Bob for squashing that fiasco and also thankful to him for getting me out of the middle of a mess. I couldn't imagine facing the loser, or being blamed for what the "instigators" really would have caused. Bob shook hands with Charles again at the wedding reception. "Take good care of her," he said.

Remember now, by then I'm only 18 and Charles was only a year and a half older. In retrospect, we were really too young to be married in the first place. Yet I still did not investigate his background. I probably should have, because after the wedding, I found out that most of the things he had told me about himself were not true. He had two children; didn't graduate from high school; and although he had a good job, it wasn't at the prestigious place where he had claimed. He did get promoted to foreman though. So it didn't really matter because he made enough money to take care of both of us. He said that he felt those lies were necessary to enable him to date me, for some reason. Yet because of the lies and other problems, we separated and went home to our parents, four times, before I saw my first boyfriend again, which made me wonder if I should have married the "other" man.

By that time, Bob had joined the marines, and was guarding the White House in Washington, D.C.

He looked so handsome in his dressy blue and reds with the white hat. Once he did call our house. The call shocked my husband, but he did let me speak to Bob. I made an effort to stop by his mothers' house on the way home from class after that call. That's where I saw all the pictures of him in his uniform. He had given them to his mother. Just as with all of the boxing trophies, I always wished that I could have at least one picture. I was married though and he had called just to tell me that he was engaged to be married himself. For once, he wanted to tell me in person about another woman. I simply told him to send me an invitation as he had told me to send him one when I got married.

   After that, but not because of that, Charles and I separated again for six whole months; and then reconciled. Yet, both of us found ourselves wondering why we got back together. I was again unhappily sitting around just waiting for Charles to give me another excuse to move out. One time we separated when he made a pass at one of my two bridesmaids. The last time we separated, he made a pass at the other one. There really was no blatant excuse this time, though. He was behaving to indicate that a change was needed. Honestly, we both had just lost interest. So we just mutually ended our marriage, as friends. Besides, he had met his soon to be second wife during the six-month separation anyway, and I had also gotten another marriage proposal from someone else. This time I did not take the ring. I backed out of that relationship after I realized how I was still very young. Nineteen was too young to be marrying for a second time.

So that's when I returned to try marriage with the first "too young" mistake. I guess we both wanted to make sure we were really ready to move on with someone else. This last time, we separated after only four months of reconciliation. I did not want to try it again. So I filed for a divorce. Right before we separated for the final time is when I met "The Scorpion".

He still "rags" me today for telling him that I was married and refusing to leave the nightclub with him. I must admit that I made sure that I got his attention purposely so he would want to be introduced to me. Then I went home, even though I knew my marriage was over.

I didn't see the Scorpion again though, until six months later. Charles remarried a few months after the divorce was final. It was around that same time when I received my wedding invitation in the mail from my first love. The ceremony was going to be far away out of state, so I couldn't attend the wedding. I still remember the pain I felt when I read the card. Fortunately, the pain didn't linger because I was preoccupied at the time, so I tried to shake it off. But subconsciously, the invitation had a numbing impact on me. I got shaken back into to present thoughts when I went into the lounge on campus, threw the invitation and envelope onto a window sill, forgetting that I had stuck my entire, cashed paycheck inside of it.

Instead of it just landing on the sill, it hit the wood frame, bounced up a few inches and went out of a hole in the screen. The lounge was five floors up from the ground, so the money fluttered through the air all the way down five stories to the construction workers below. I screamed! Then a classmate and I ran to the elevators and went down to recover the money. Luckily we found every cent, including the change. Laughing in disbelief, we got back upstairs just in time for class.

By then, I felt that my life was full and looking positive. I was working part-time and going to school fulltime. Also, at that time I had forgotten about the Scorpion and I was being pursued by an intelligent and handsome classmate. So I "had to be" happy for Bob's nuptials. He had really moved on.

It was also a good thing that six months earlier I had met the Scorpion. That one night gave me a dose of confidence that had been robbed from me. I still remember how he moved into my life. My friends called me and told me about a new dance club to which they had been going. They wanted me to go with them on Thursday. Thursday was the night when our favorite DJ spun records at the club. He always provided music for our social club dances. All of our friends followed him to wherever he DJ'd. Because my husband Charles didn't dance, he usually declined invitations to dances, discos, parties, and clubs. Remember, we have just mistakenly reunited after a 6-month separation of dating other people. So, he didn't really care what I did that night and I didn't really care what he did. I still extended the courtesy of asking him if he wanted to go or not.

I remember my exact words: "Charles, I'm going to the new club with my friends on Thursday, do you want to go with me?"

"No. You know I don't dance and I'm not a club person," he unsurprisingly said.

"Your friends will probably be there too," I pleaded.

He repeated, "No. You go ahead. I have to go to work tomorrow anyway."

Then I was really thinking about how drab and spark-less our marriage was and how he'd not even really tried to get the spark back, even though he kept asking me to come back every time he saw me. He also still had my name tattooed on his arm. Yet his "just being there", was depressing and frustrating. It was strange because we had just moved into a beautiful new apartment, but we were both miserable. The fun we once had in our marriage was truly "all gone".

That Thursday night came and I started to get dressed. "You sure you don't want to go Charles?" I asked.

"I'm sure," he answered.

"Do you mind if I go?" I asked noticing the expression on his face.

He replied again, "No. You go ahead."

Even though I felt his pain, I went anyway. It was the same pain that I felt when we broke up. Breaking up/divorcing is hard to do, even if your feelings are numb. Yet, I went to the club, had fun and did not worry about Charles.

Chapter 2:
MEETING SWEET SCORPION

When I got to the club, I felt so good dancing. It was as if I were releasing the tension that had piled up at home. I had been having headaches everyday. My headache was starting to go away after I began dancing. I noticed the relief and kept dancing, letting it all hang out. Then that's when I noticed the "Scorpion". He was a very nice-looking guy, with a perfect afro. It was a naturally curly afro and cut very neatly. Plus he had thick long eyelashes to go with his pretty eyes. He had caramel brown skin and a demeanor that didn't appear to be cocky, egomaniacal, or overconfident. I knew a lot of people, but I had never seen this guy before. I saw him constantly looking my way. So I twirled in the middle of the dance floor. As I did, the DJ saw me and started saying my name, "Erin's in the house. Go Erin. Go Erin. Go Erin." I was already trying to make sure the Scorpion noticed me. So, the DJ's acknowledgement definitely helped.

When the song was over, I watched the Scorpion with my peripheral vision, but I didn't let him see me watching. I could see that he was looking at me, too. "Yes!" I later noticed him talking to some of the same friends that had invited me out that night. He must have seen me with them and was asking them who I was. It was standing room only, and when they returned to our huddle, I asked about him as they told me he wanted to meet me. Surprisingly, he went to the same college that they did.

"Hi, I'm Jordan," he said when he approached me.

"I'm Erin," I said.

"How is it that I've never seen you before? You don't go to our school, do you?" he asked.

"No. I'm in a 2-year surgical tech program at the hospital."

"So does that mean you must be very straight-forward – sort of an organized type of person? What sign are you?" Jordan asked.

"Gemini," I replied. "What about you?"

"Scorpio," he said with a smile that swept me off my feet.

"You don't sting, do you?" I teased.

"That's what Scorpions do, isn't it?" he teased back. "Gemini is my favorite sign. They are always sweet," he smiled.

"We're friendly, free-spirited people when you get to know us," I said.

"Right," he retorted in a cunning way, "and Scorpions are sweet too."

We started laughing and constantly talking. As we walked toward the door he introduced me to his friend. "Jeremy. This is Erin. Erin, this is Jeremy. "

"Hi," I said.

"Nice to meet you," Jeremy replied.

"Want to take a ride with me?" Jordan asked.

"No. I can't. I'm married and I need to get home."

"Oh, married?"

"Yes." We both reached for the door. "Yet it was nice meeting you," I said and quickly got into the car with my friends.

Leaning over on the door, he whispered, "Just remember that my name is Jordan. I'm not a real Scorpion, but I can be a predator when I like the prey that I see."

"Then maybe you'll see me again someday," I teased. My friends and I drove off and I did not see him again for a while.

In the meantime, December came. Charles and I had been together four months, during an unhappy reconciliation. "What's the matter?" I asked, as Charles walked into the door from work one evening.

"My car broke down and I had to get a ride home," he said angrily.

"Can you get the car fixed? How are you going to get to work?" I asked.

"My friends will pick me up, but you will need a ride to school and back."

"Maybe I should stay at my mom's until you get the car fixed, since she lives near the school." I felt happy to make the suggestion.

"Good idea. Eric is on the way over. Maybe he can drop you at your Mom's on his way home."

I quickly picked up the phone to call and then packed to wait for Eric. A few days of peace went by, with me at my mom's. My headaches must have been stress-related because they seemed to go away. Later on that week, I called Charles to see if the car was ready. "How are you doing?" I asked.

"Fine," he said. "What about you?"

"I'm ok. How's the car?" I hesitantly asked.

"It will be ready tomorrow," he said.

"You know, I was thinking of staying here for a while," I said hoping for agreement and feedback.

"I was thinking that too," he said.

"I'm glad we both are honest and are in agreement," I said, relieved.

"Me too," he said.

"I want to come and pick up some more of my things tomorrow, if that's ok?"

"OK!" he said. "I'll see you then." Eric picked me up on his way to Charles' the next evening. In the back of my mind, my thought was "so I could pack all of my things." When we knocked on the door, Charles opened it.

"Hi", he said, "Come on in. Sue our next door neighbor is here cooking me one of her favorite dishes. She didn't think you would mind."

"Hi Sue," I said, glad that he was moving on quickly.

"Hi," she said to Eric and me. "Would you like something to eat?"

"No thanks," Eric and I both said in unison.

"I won't be here too long. I just want to gather my things."

Charles, Eric, and I walked down to the car with my things. "You work pretty fast there, Charles," I laughed.

"Yeah, dawg. You didn't even wait 'til her clothes were gone," Eric said, laughing too.

"What can I say?" Charles said laughing with us.

"Ya'll sure ya'll don't want to rethink this?" Eric asked.

"We both know what we're doing Eric. Let's go, so he can get back to his guest," I smiled as I got into the car.

"I can't believe that you guys don't even sleep together anymore, uh, not with a body like yours," Eric grinned.

"Yeah, well, believe it, and keep your eyes on the road," I insisted, making sure that he wasn't flirting.

"Besides, his mind is probably on that girl he was dating last summer. I'm old news now. She is the new novelty," I said with a peaceful thought of "no more headaches."

It was my last year at the surgical tech school and I was working steadily part-time hours after school at the hospital. My divorce had been filed, would be paid for, and would be final in six months. Besides, I was dating again and life seemed so much more peaceful. I was feeling happy and free. My 21st birthday would be in the spring and I would graduate a few months after that. Life was good.

The new guy that I was dating was one of my med tech classmates. Angelo was very quiet and nice. He also was very handsome, yet with a baby face. He and I were the youngest in our class and we were known for giggling and dancing a lot.

"He's too quiet," one of my old friends from high school said, as we entered the house party to which we were invited.

"He doesn't even smoke cigarettes," she said. This was a surprise coming from her because she didn't smoke and neither did I. I guess she thought it was a manly thing. I was thinking to myself, "That's the reason I like him." I grabbed his hand as he smiled.

Charles had said that I had more in common with the new guy than with him and he thought we had the same personality and character traits. Charles was really just approving and being honest with himself and me because he was about to set the date to marry the girl he had dated last summer.

"Why did you call my mom? I was only kidding," Charles said when I called him later during the week.

"Your brothers go to school with Angelo's sisters. They said you sent a message that you might jump on him. I called your mother so she could make sure you behave," I said.

"You know I was just kidding. I knew they all go to school together. His mom lives around the corner from my mom. Tell him that I was just joking around and that I think that you and he make a nice couple. He's a nice, quiet person and you have more in common with him than you do with me," he said.

"Why did you move back home to your mom's anyway?" I asked.

"My mom's attic was empty and I don't have to pay rent here. Why keep the apartment?"

"You could have had yourself a bachelor's pad," I said.

"I've got a bachelor's pad right here," he laughed.

"I knew that was what you would do," I said, knowing that his overbearing mother would talk him into moving home. I even had trouble convincing them we were going to live in our own place when we got married.

My new friend, Angelo and I worked part-time after school at the hospital five days a week. We were halfway through our second year and nearing graduation. Working four hours a night after school was a requirement, but the head of the school always, intentionally scheduled Angelo and I on different shifts. If I worked 4:00 P.M. to 8:00 P.M., he worked 8:00 P.M. to 12:00 midnight. We didn't live very far from the hospital so it didn't cost us much gas, but it separated us for eight hours a day. I never left his side any other time. We didn't officially live together, but he had a separate space at his mother's house that I never left. I'd go to the kitchen to help his sisters with dinner or to help wash dishes, just to show him that I was strong enough to leave his side, but I was always right there in the house somewhere.

Unfortunately, occasionally his high school sweetheart would call there and talk to his entire family one-by-one, while I was there. He convinced me though that she had a new boyfriend, maybe even a husband. Besides, she had just had a baby. So I didn't worry too much. There were a couple of other callers such as a neighbor, another high school friend, and an old tenant of his grandmother's. The high school sweetheart was the only one that seemed to have a special place in everyone's heart. Oh well, he was always with me and I had never been so happy.

One night though, while I was working the 8 to 12 shift, I called Angelo about 10:00 P.M., but he wasn't there. His family owned apartment buildings, so I figured he had gone to one of those places to get it ready for renting. I called again at 11:00 P.M. He still wasn't there. When it was time for me to get off work, I was paranoid, hurt, and upset. Now I knew better than to appear as a neurotic, desperate chic to a man's family, but I think I called every hour on the hour until I got him around 2:00 A.M. I had told myself that I was just paranoid because I had been at the hospital since 7:00 A.M. I had to be just tired.

When I talked to him though, he told me the truth. My woman's intuition and "paranoia" was right on the money. He was with another woman. His high school sweetheart had gotten upset with her baby's daddy and stopped by Angelo's mother's to ask him to go out for a drink with her. He just couldn't say no to the woman that he had once loved so dearly. When I woke up the next morning, I kept thinking that I wasn't paranoid, I wasn't just tired. What if she decided she wanted him back? I walked around for two days trying to hide my true feelings. I knew I was tripping because I never thought we would ever break up. But now I had to realize that it was possible, even though he was trying to convince me that it wasn't.

The third day came around and I had to pinch myself. "I am not married to this man, and I am not going to let this drive me crazy," I told myself. I called my friends from the junior college and told them to "find that guy" to whom they had introduced me. "Give him my phone number!" I insisted. I needed someone to fall back on – a balance to keep me from whining and crying to Angelo, and to myself.

When Jordan finally called, I felt my strength come back. Yep, after a few days of talking to my new Scorpion friend, I felt that Angelo could go out with anybody. The pain would bounce off me and I could handle it.

Angelo behaved after that, and I wasn't at my mom's enough to get Jordan's few phone calls anyway. A few weeks went by. I missed many of the Scorpion's calls because I was glued to Angelo's side as before. However, it meant a lot, just knowing my new friend had called my mom's house. I still needed to keep my strength. Then one day, when I was talking to my family on the phone, and Angelo heard me ask who had called. That's when he started asking questions.

"You've been staying at your mom's more often than you use to. Who are you expecting to call you there?" he asked.

I told him the truth. "I do have a friend that calls me occasionally, but it's no big deal," I said defensively. I was starting to feel a little too relaxed and unattached. I started missing those phone calls though. I did decide to call Jordan whenever I could, but he was never at home. I remember that he had told me he lived with his mother. So I figured that he must have been hanging out with his friends from school most of the time. Then I did get that long-awaited phone call one day after school.

"I'm tired of talking to you on the phone. When can I see you?" Jordan asked.

"I have a boyfriend, you know," I responded.

"And?"

"And, I'm trying, everyday, to keep it together." I did not know where I wanted my relationship with Jordan to go.

"Well, where is he at now?" he asked.

"He's at work now and I have to be there at 8:00 P.M."

"How are you getting there?"

"I don't know. I guess my dad will drop me off."

"How about I come over and take you?" he asked.

"I don't know about that. Angelo gets off work when I go in to work. I'm not comfortable with that."

"What are you doing now?"

"Just relaxing until I have to go in."

"I'll be there in a few minutes, OK?" he insisted.

"OK," I said.

"So why are you still with this guy?" Jordan asked, as I motioned for him to sit down in my parents' living room.

"Well. So far he only once went out with this girl since we've been together, as far as I know. She calls occasionally, but he says she has a man and a baby." Even knowing that, I wondered what kind of man her new man was like, since mine was worth returning to. I also wondered, but did not wonder aloud, if she was thinking of making a final comeback.

"So you think he might behave?" Jordan asked.

"Maybe. He was honest about where he was. I guess. We'll see. Let's change the subject anyway. Tell me more about you. Have you ever been married? Do you have any kids?" I asked, trying to keep my mind clear of worrying about Angelo's actions.

"No, I've never been married, and no I don't have any children," he said, making me think he was much too sophisticated and intelligent to get himself involved like that before finishing college. Just then a horn blew.

"That's my friend Carlos. We can take you to work. Come on, it'll be okay," he said.

"OK. Let me get my lab coat and purse." I went to the back to tell my mom I was leaving. After that day, Jordan and Carlos would drop me off at work at least once a week, right before Angelo's shift ended. One day while Angelo was at work, Jordan called and was glad to find out that I was off that night.

"Good, he said. I'll pick you up and we can go for a ride or something," he said. I was very nervous, but I tried not to show it as I got into the car. He was very refined and sophisticated. He opened the door for me. Then he closed it behind me. I could tell that he had good home training just as Angelo, but I was Angelo's classmate for a whole year before we even thought about dating each other. That gave me plenty of time to get to know him and be comfortable around him. This was different. There was something about Jordan that made me nervous. I had to go potty every time I got into the car with him. It was almost similar to stepping on a Scorpion that didn't sting and you knew he would, but I wondered why he did not.

For the first time that night, we were by ourselves in his car. Maybe that's what made my nervousness worst. I was so frazzled and it became very obvious. We were just talking and I hesitated without saying anything right in the middle of our conversation.

"What's wrong?" he asked.

"I – I got to go pee. Oops. I can't believe I said that," I said as he started laughing; so I started laughing too.

"I can't believe I said that," I said again shaking my head.

"Why? If you've got to go, you've got to go," he said still laughing. He drove me to his brother's house to use the bathroom. We sat around for a while afterwards and then he took me home.

Later, he started coming over more often. By then the weather was getting warmer. We would normally shoot pool in my parent's basement and shoot the breeze a lot. "Now," I thought, "he's really a perfect gentleman. He's not trying to get intimate with me at all and he doesn't seem to mind that I'm still with Angelo." He was a perfect friend, a perfect balance; and the strength I needed to be with Angelo. Then something dangerous happened.

He came by my Mom's on another one of my off days. We were just riding around and suddenly without warning, he said "Oops!" He ducked his head down, quickly turned the corner, and also pushed my head down.

"What's up?" I brazenly asked as I noticed him looking through the rear view mirror.

"Uh, it's my girlfriend. This is her car and if she sees me with you in here, I don't know what she'll do. She might shoot you or something."

"What?" I said. "First, I thought this was Carlos' car since he was always driving. Then you had been picking me up by yourself lately, so I thought it was your car. Now, you tell me I've been riding around in your girlfriend's car?" I shook my head in disgust. I knew then that I was really starting to like him too much.

"She's really the emotional type. Her husband was killed in Vietnam and left her with a little baby boy to rear by herself. She's really fragile," he said to me as if he wanted me to understand.

"I thought you said you didn't sting like a Scorpion? What's up with this? That hurts. Come to think of it, is she why you're never home when I call your mom's house?"

"I do have a room at my mom's house, but I have a room a Judy's house too," he said.

"I think you'd better take me home before you get me shot or something," I said.

"I thought he was too fine to be free for real," I said to myself. "I should have known better." Who really cared though? I had Angelo and we kind of had the same arrangement at his mother's house.

When I got home I started thinking about the day when Jordan had come over with scratches on his face and neck. He had brushed it off as nothing. Now I'm wondering if that "nothing" that I thought was a fight with a male, was actually a fight with a female - Judy. When Angelo got off work that night, I went home with him, where I thought I probably belonged, anyway.

Jordan called me a few days later while I was at my Mom's house. He asked me if he could come over. "We can still be friends. We were friends when I knew you had a boyfriend," he said.

"Yea, ok," I said hesitantly. I knew that he was right.

The "hen pecked" song was playing on the radio by the time he came. "She plays that song over and over, all the time," he said as we played pool in the basement.

"Well there is nothing wrong with giving your woman respect. I like that song, too. You must care about her. You still live with her," I said.

"I love her. I really do, but I want my freedom. I want to do whatever I want to do, whenever I want to do it," he insisted.

"Is that where those scratches came from?" I finally asked.

"Yea, well", he said, shrugging his shoulders." She does that rolling arms windmill thing, and crying, when she thinks I'm not behaving."

"I don't know what to say," I said, knowing I was once in a relationship in which I had to figure how to end it; and I've been in her place also trying to make somebody act right and reciprocate love in the same manner that it was giving.

"Don't say anything. Let's change the subject. Tell me, why is your brother always coming down stairs when I'm over here? I might want to kiss you one day, or something. Is he guarding his little sister, or what?" he smiled.

"I never thought it bothered you," I said surprised he even mentioned kissing me. He'd never tried to kiss me in all this time. Now I was surprised and curious about him.

"You've probably got hair on your chest don't you?" I asked as I moved closer to him, loosened a button on his shirt and looked down to see if he had hair on his chest as pretty as the hair on his head.

"What are you doing?" he smiled and asked.

"I want to see the hair on your chest," I teased. We both laughed, as I surprised myself again by being so flirtatious.

Right on cue though, I heard my brother walking downstairs. We kept shooting pool. This time he only stayed and talked to us for a short time. So when I got ready to drive myself to work, Jordan was able to kiss me goodbye. He started coming over almost every day after that. It did not matter to him whether Angelo was on his way or not.

"You're going to get me in trouble with Angelo," I said one day.

"So what? You should be mine anyway," he said as he pulled me closer to him.

"Why do you like me?" I asked.

"You go to school, you work, you don't have any babies, and you don't wear a ton of make-up," he complemented. "Why do you like me?"

"Who said I like you?" I laughed as I pretended to pull away. He grabbed me and again pulled me closer to him.

"OK," I said laughing. "You're fun, and I like you."

"A lot?" he asked.

"Yes. A lot," I said.

"I don't have any children and you don't either. Why don't you have a baby with me?" he asked.

"No way! You're not really ready for a baby. I'm not finished with school yet, and its time for you to go," I said, thinking that being somebody's first and only baby's mama, did sound good. What about the marriage part? He didn't say anything about that, and he's not finished with school yet either.

"I'm not ready to go yet," he said, kissing me for a long time.

"Goodbye," I said, breaking away. I pulled him up the stairs. He hesitated and I had to beg him to leave again.

My dad was near the doorway after Jordan left. So, he saw Angelo's car. "You're playing with fire," my dad said.

"I know," I told my dad, "but Jordan refuses to leave sometimes. He says I should be his girlfriend, not Angelo's."

"Do you like him?" my dad asked.

"I do like him, but I don't know who I like the most," I said as I went to open the door for Angelo.

"Just be careful," my dad advised. For once I saw a deep concern as he walked into the kitchen. Soon after that close encounter, Jordan talked me into skipping school so we could spend an entire day together and forget that we had any other commitments. I agreed. We laughed and played. We truly enjoyed each other's company all day. Then I didn't hear from him for a couple of weeks. I thought this was odd after he had been bugging me for so long, and at the same time dodging Angelo every day for months.

"Where have you been?" I asked when he finally called.

"You know why you're sounding possessive all of sudden, don't you?" he asked, sounding as if he were smiling.

"OK. You're right, but where have you been?" I asked, feeling kind of foolish.

"I've been around. Can I come over right now?" he asked.

"Yes," I said happily, but hesitantly thinking that I should have said no. By then it was too late to say no. Jordan began coming over regularly again. Things began to get heated and eventually kissing was not the only thing that we did.

"Um-umh. This is the third pair of underwear I've had to throw away over here," he said. "If I keep coming over here, I'm going to have to buy a new set every week," he said, kissing me. He threw that pair in the outside dumpster and drove off as I thought to myself "his bikinis aren't pink, but they are prettier than mine."

Life suddenly changed for me though. One day as Angelo and I were sitting in the living room at my mother's house, the phone rang. My mother yelled that it was for me. "Hello," I said.

"Uh, hi. Erin?" the female voice asked.

"Hi," I said trying to picture the face to which the voice belonged.

"This is Judy," she said, very nicely and sweet-like. "I hope you don't mind, but I found your number in Jordan's wallet and I just wanted to know where I stand with him. I don't want to keep wasting my time. You know what I mean?" she asked, still being very nice.

"Well Judy, I have a boyfriend," I said. "In fact he's sitting right here with me now."

"Do you think Jordan cares about me as much as he does you?" she asked.

"Look Judy, Jordan and I are good friends. Jordan told me that he really loves you." I refused to tell her the rest. It wasn't my place to tell her that he said he wanted his freedom.

"Thank you. I hope you understand. I just needed to know if I was being foolish or not," she said.

"Oh brother," I said as I hung up. "What a sad mess."

Angelo looked at me and asked, "What's going on?"

"That was my new friend's girlfriend. You know the person that I told you who calls me every now and then. She wanted to know if he loves her or not," I said shaking my head.

"You know I've been feeling his presence a lot lately too. What is going on between you two?" a little annoyed, Angelo asked.

"I'm going to be honest with you. I don't know what I'm feeling anymore. Maybe we do need a break for a while," I said.

The next day at school Angelo and I talked briefly. "You know. There's a girl here at the hospital that a couple of the guys were telling me about. She's a nursing student and they say she wants to go out with me. Do you mind if I go?" Angelo asked.

"I don't mind. Have fun. My emotions are so mixed up now. Yea, let's take a break for a minute," I said.

That evening as I was walking down the street to my mom's from the store, a car pulled up beside me.

"We should kidnap her, don't you think?" I heard a voice say. I usually ignore men flirting with me when I'm walking down the street, but the voices sounded familiar. I looked around. It was Jordan and his best friend Jeremy. I smiled and got into the car.

We drove back to my mom's where we talked and laughed for a few minutes.

"My birthday is next week," I said.

"Maybe I'll come get you, and take you out to the club where we met," he winked. What day is your birthday?"

"Wednesday," I said.

"Ok. I'll be here around 8:00 P.M. Be ready, okay," he smiled.

"OK," I said.

At school the next day, Angelo told me about his date with the nursing student.

"I went out with Bambi last night," he said.

"Did you have fun?" I asked.

"Yeah, she was okay. She told all of the guys that she really likes me," he said, as if he was not sure he should have taken her out.

"I can understand why she likes you. Now what?" I asked.

"That's up to you!" He threw the burden back on me. "Where's your head at? What about what's-his-name?" he asked.

"I don't know. Let's just take it slow. See how things go…" After that conversation we clung together as usual. When Wednesday came, Angelo gave me my birthday presents, and then I remembered I had a date. I asked Angelo for permission to go though. I drove to my mom's. Jordan drove up just as I did and saw that I had on jeans.

"You're not dressed to go out. What's up with that?" he asked very annoyed. "And why did you tell Judy that I loved her? Now that she thinks I love her, we will never break up! To top it off, you're not the only girl she called. One of the stupid girls cussed her out for calling. Why didn't you?" he asked, very upset.

"Well, you did tell me you loved her. I wasn't going to tell her the rest. She seemed very nice. Why would I cuss her out when all she wanted to know is where she stood with you, so she wouldn't be wasting her time. I probably would have done the same thing - asked to be told the truth. What's up with you? How many other girls are there?" I asked, wondering where they were when he was over here everyday, bugging me.

"What do you mean, how many other girls? I'm talking about when she called Fontana. Fontana cussed her out. She found her name in my wallet just like she found yours and one other girl too," he said, still annoyed.

"Who's Fontana?" I questioned, since he said her name as if he had already told me about her.

"Oh, I forgot. She's the girl who lost my twins. She's the only girl that's ever been pregnant by me. I told you that I didn't have any children. She almost died during the miscarriage. Anyway, she cussed Judy out for calling. You probably should have done the same. Now I don't know what to do," he said.

"I'm not the one wasting her time. You're the one who's supposed to tell her the truth. Don't change the subject anyway. Why did this, uh, Fontana, cuss Judy out? Judy didn't talk crazy to me?" I asked wondering what else he hadn't told me.

"Fontana has always hated that she lost the babies. She still loved me, but she had two kids by this other dude already, and she decided she had better go back to him, since I probably wasn't going to marry her without my kids," he said.

"Now Judy has set off this 'Fontana' girl's ego, and she may want to come back, now that she knows she has competition," I thought to myself. I was in such shock though, that I could only shake my head and say, "What a mess!"

"What a mess? Yeah, thanks a lot. I'll talk to you later," he said angrily as he walked out of the door to meet Jeremy at the bottom of the steps.

I was so pissed that I just got into my car and drove back to Angelo's. I passed Jordan and Jeremy along the way as they walked from my mom's to Jordan's brother-in-law's job down the street. I blew at them as Jordan pointed a finger at me and shook his head. I guess Jordan was pretty pissed at me too, for doing what was right, I thought. I didn't hear from him for a couple of months. Meanwhile, back at school, Angelo's new friend was bugging out and bugging me. I realize that she and her friends must have been the ones my mom's neighbor overheard talking when the neighbor was a patient at the hospital.

"That Angelo is one fine man," she heard them say. "But that Erin is always walking around here holding his hand so nobody else can get to him."

I had no other options. Things were now bad with Jordan. They didn't get any better about Angelo at work either. "Bambi has been calling here every five minutes for you Angelo," Susan, one of our classmates said, as Angelo and I walked into the surgical department together.

"Yeah, we told her that you hadn't gotten here yet, but she keeps calling back. That's probably her on the phone again, now."

"Mary," another attendant said answering the phone. I walked towards the phone.

"You want to talk to her, Angelo?" I asked being tired and not being in the mood for drama.

"No, not right now," he said.

"Hello. Surgical department. Erin speaking," I said.

"Is Angelo there?" she asked.

"Who's speaking?" I demanded.

"It's Bambi", she said.

"Bambi. He says he doesn't feel like talking right now," I said, exercising my "I'm his girlfriend" rights.

Angelo looked at me and shook his head, saying "Oh, brother."

I hung up, and our friends started laughing. "We're going to breakfast," I told everyone, just in case someone wanted to know. Angelo and I got on the elevator and went to the cafeteria. We put our breakfast on our trays, found a table, and sat down to eat. Guess who showed up? Bambi and a couple of her friends walked in to get their breakfast too. Instead of sitting somewhere else, they came and sat at our table, straight across from me and Angelo.

"So you didn't want to talk to me this morning, Angelo?" Bambi asked.

"I was a little busy in the department," Angelo said diplomatically.

"Yeah, I see," she said rolling her eyes across to me. "He wasn't too busy to talk to me the other night," she said to me.

"Yeah, well today is a new day," I shrugged.

"She's going to beat you up," Angelo jokingly whispered to me.

"You better not let her," I softly whispered back.

"So are you back together with her, Angelo?" she asked angrily.

"I really don't know," he admitted. "What are we going to do?" Angelo turned to me and seriously asked for an answer.

"I don't know if we're getting back together or not," I said looking at Bambi. "I'm still thinking about it!"

Instead of Angelo just letting it go, he continued. "Well, I would like to know."

"She knew you had a woman in the first place. So she's going to have to wait until we decide whether we're going to be together or not," I said to both him and her. "Is that ok with you?" I asked turning to him.

"OK with me", he said smiling. She got the message, then got up and moved as Angelo and I finished our breakfast.

Even though I should have been making a decision, I must admit that every time the doorbell rang at my mom's I was wishing it would have been Jordan. It never was. I refused to chase him, so I didn't try to call him. Angelo and I were still together, although things weren't really the same. Then one day he found a note on my car that was left by one of my old high school friends.

"I found this note on your car. Is this a new boyfriend?" Angelo said.

"Does the note say he's my boyfriend?" I asked, knowing this was the same guy my friends thought I was with before, but I wasn't. "He just found out what my new car looks like. He's just a family friend. His mom's house is right over the back fence from the hospital. His mom works for this hospital too," I said, wondering why people always kept thinking that he and I had a thing for each other. Back in those days, I didn't think it was normal, human, or feminine to be without a boyfriend, but I had no thoughts of being with anyone, even though I knew that Angelo and I were fading. Besides, I thought about my disappearing Scorpion all the time, but I knew I had to give up on him. There were the thoughts of having a new car, turning 21, my divorce finalized, and my fast approaching graduation date.

All of those things were giving me the urge to truly embrace and enjoy being independent, unattached, and free. I knew that I had to let Angelo go too, so I could enjoy that feeling, without guilt. He thought that we should stay together at least until after we studied and took our boards (and he was probably right), but I ended it anyway.

Then one night when I was sitting on my mom's porch with a bunch of my friends, my note-writing pen pal, Maynard, drove up with a brand new Lincoln, the same color as my new Mustang. For a change I was boyfriend-less, which was probably a good thing. Unfortunately, my match-making friends didn't think so.

"He has a car the same color as yours and both of ya'll got good jobs. That's a sign," they said.

As soon as I decided that it might be alright to date him and was sitting in his car in front of my mom's, guess who finally came walking down the street to visit me? After two months of me wishing he'd show up, he did. The added negative bonus was that Maynard and Jordan knew each other.

"I shouldn't have changed my mind about becoming a nun," I thought. I wanted to be a nun until 5th grade, when I decided that marrying one of my classmates was a better idea. Right then I knew that I should have gone to the convent.

Jordan and Jeremy started laughing and shooting the breeze with my new friend Maynard. I just sat there, not believing that Jordan showed up now, after I had really decided to move on. He even showed up again the next day and tried to kiss me. I backed up saying, "Oh no, it's too late now."

"Oh, now that you've got a new boyfriend, you're off limits", he said smiling.

"That's right," I said. "Where's Judy anyway?" I asked.

"I messed up. So she finally gave up. Then Tori came and told me that she had a new boyfriend. Instead of saying "good", I took myself over to her house and confronted her about having a boyfriend. What did I do that for? Now she really thinks that I love her and can't do without her," he said shaking his head.

"So why did you do that?" I asked.

"Silly, I guess," he said laughing, but still shaking his head at himself. "You know, your new boyfriend has been bragging to everybody that he's taken one of my gals from me. Jeremy is really pissed and wants to confront him about it," he said as I shook my head.

"No. Don't start anything."

"Yeah, I told him not to worry about it. He wasn't too convinced he should let it go, but he's okay for now," he said.

"How many gals do you have anyway?" I asked.

"Ah baby. You know when I talk, I mean my ex's and things," he said smiling.

"Yeah. I bet," I said. I was so glad he was there, but I kept wondering where all the women came from all of a sudden. I didn't see Jordan again for a while until one Sunday Charles, my first husband, showed up, a week before his wedding to his 2nd wife. Then Jordan arrived right after Charles. I introduced them to each other. They shook hands. My mom had bar-b-qued that day for some reason. They both stayed. They both ate.

"I've heard of him," Charles said when Jordan went to the bathroom. "He should give me some respect for being your first husband, right?"

"Yeah, I guess so," I said, not sure what that meant. I guess that meant that they could be friends without animosity - and they could. It was a pleasant day. Maynard, my new friend, was different from both of them, though. He loved to explore different avenues. We would go to the Watermelon Man Café and eat watermelon on the patio, the Lobster House, the Steak House, or eat pig ear sandwiches off the pig ear truck. We went up to the top of the Gateway Arch in that tiny little crawl-in elevator. He wanted to take me on a helicopter ride around the city too. We never got around to that, though. I'm surprised he didn't ask me to go bungee jumping. He did pick me up from work on a motorcycle one day when I let him borrow my car, while his was being serviced. I wasn't thrilled about the motorcycle. I was a hospital worker, mainly in the emergency room (ER). We're not usually very fond of motorcycles because of the disasters we've seen. Other than that, Maynard and I had a lot of fun, until he asked me to move in with him. I should have taken heed to the first warning. He told me to meet him at his mom's after work one night. When I arrived, his brother and two of his male friends were there waiting for him, too. We all sat outside on the porch, cracking jokes for about an hour.

Somebody finally said, "Uh, you think he's going to show up?"

"It is getting late. It's 1:15 A.M.," his friend Marvin said.

"He'll be here," his brother said. "He lives here."

"Well, ok," I added. We continued to wait. When 2:15 A.M. came around, I said my goodbyes and went home. The next evening, the guys came by and told me what happened. Maynard had said that I was crowding him, and that he needed some air.

"Oh wow," I said surprised. "What am I suppose to say to that?"

"Don't know. He's tripping, but it'll be alright," they tried to convince me.

I tried not to ever call him after that. Instead, I let him contact me when he wanted us to go out. A couple of weeks later he was admitted into the hospital by his doctor. I still did not call. So he called and asked me to bring him a radio. When I got there, I saw a young lady leaving as I was entering. Of course, I'm not certain, but I think it was his son's mother. They had one child together. He was named after Maynard. She had four other children, though, so he said that they were no longer together. Surprisingly, when he got out of the hospital, he still wanted us to go look for a place and some furniture.

That's when we resumed a normal relationship. Of course, I called Jordan, when I was told that Maynard needed me to give him some 'air'. It took a while for Jordan's mom to get the message to him. At that time, he still didn't live with her. When he did come by, I told him that Maynard and I were looking for a spot. We had looked in the same place where I heard he and Judy were still hanging out.

"So you might be my neighbor?" he asked.

"I hope not. I don't think that will be a good idea," I said seriously. I'm pretty strong about being monogamous and overly sensitive when it comes to letting a man know that I won't cheat on him. Seriously, I was afraid of the buttons Maynard might push, living around the wrong guy."

"What's the matter? You afraid you might sneak over to my place?" Jordan laughed. Later Maynard and I settled on an apartment in the city that was closer to our jobs. Except for the new refrigerator and stove I got on my Penney's charge card, we bought second-hand furniture from newspaper ads. It was a good thing too, because all the fun we were having, ended as soon as we moved in together. We hardly ever went out and when he was at home, he and his friends would pass out drunk on my couch. If I wanted them to go home, I had to take them, in the middle of the night, because Maynard couldn't drive.

I remember thinking one Sunday, "I grew up with both parents going to church every Sunday. This is not what I expected of a relationship." The church was right down the street from our apartment.

"Would you start going to church with me?" I asked Maynard.

"No. Sunday's my resting day," he said.

So I started going by myself, wondering, "What am I doing in this relationship, and when am I going to tell him I'm moving out?"

One day Maynard called me from his mom's house. He had been standing on the block with our friends when my first boyfriend, Bob, showed up. He had brought his new bride home to meet the rest of his family who didn't travel to the wedding in D.C.

"Anybody seen Erin?" he had asked.

Everybody got real quiet. So Maynard piped in, "Uh, she's with me now. We have an apartment on Pope Avenue," he said.

Maynard must have had to run around to his mom's, because he called me from there and said that Bob exploded and threatened him. Then Maynard said, "His cock-strong ass better not jump me."

"Maynard, just calm down. He's just messing with you. You know he just got married. I'm the last thing on his mind," I said. As soon as I hung up, Bob knocked on the door. Now I'm thinking to myself, "Maynard, or one of the guys, must have told him more than what street we live on. They must have told him the exact address since he came straight to my door." I opened the door and let him in. He was calm.

"How are you doing?" he asked.

"I'm fine," I said. "How about you?" I asked. "I got your wedding invitation. Congratulations!"

"What happened to Charles?" he asked.

"We got divorced about four months ago. He just got married again, last week. How's your family?" I asked.

"Madea and everybody are fine," he said. "I just came by to see how you were doing and say hello. I'd better get back. They're cooking a big meal and everybody's there."

"OK. You take care."

"I'll probably go by your mom's and see your family before I head back to D.C. You take care babe," he said as he brushed a kiss on my forehead.

Later, Maynard came home. I thought he might get humble and behave for a few days; and he did, but not without telling me how "naturally pretty" Bob's new wife was. I guess he felt he had to hurt me or "checkmate" me while Bob was in town. After about a week, women resumed calling the apartment for Maynard. Sometimes he wouldn't even come home at all. One woman got so bold, she sent her child to the apartment with Maynard's car keys, saying he was passed out on her couch. After that, I gave Maynard a month's notice, that I was moving out even though I had only been there a month. I told him I would take the stove and fridge, and that he could have the rest.

Of course, he wanted to start wining and dining me again, so we went to a place for lobster. He usually ate something else at the Lobster House, but this night he decided to eat lobster with me, instead of steak. Before we got home he had hives all over him. My mom told me what to get him at the drugstore, and he was better the next day. He tried to behave during that month, but he really couldn't. So without further notice, after an incident with another woman, I just moved out while he was at work. I got everything of mine out, and spent the night at a friend's, so he couldn't find me at my mom's. I was working the day shift the next morning and I didn't have my white stockings to wear with my uniform. In those days, stores didn't open before 9:00 A.M. and it was 6:00 o'clock in the morning. So, since I still had the keys, I thought why not stop by and get my stockings out of the drawer where I had left them.

When I got in the door, there was Maynard and some woman lying totally in the nude, asleep in our bed. I just tip-toed around them, got my stockings, and went on to work. After seeing this, I just wanted to be free. I really didn't care anymore.

It took a couple of weeks for my apartment to get ready. My friends tried to keep me entertained. They even introduced me to a very nice looking guy. Unfortunately for me, his wife and little girl came back to him. So that never even began. I tried to call Jordan, but he was living with some girl named Elaine. Moving day finally came and it was like getting freed from slavery, almost. I was 21 years old! I had a new car, and now my own apartment. By then there were new clubs opening up everywhere. Two were on the same street where I lived. There were also two on the same street as my mom. Each club had a special night on which all my friends would meet. So we had somewhere to go every night. One night I decided to go to the club down from my mom's with my co-worker after work. I wore my winter brownish-pink knickers, a brownish pink sweater vest, and a white tie blouse that I tied into a long bow. I had on winter white stockings and some loafers, which we all wore with quarters in them instead of pennies. I had a feeling my honey was in the club, and as soon as I walked into the door, there he was with about eight of his friends. I pretended I didn't see him, as usual, but I saw him and his friends eyeing me. He tipped up on me to surprise me. As soon as he got close, to tap me on the shoulder, I jumped out of the way and turned to him.

"I'm always two steps ahead of you, Scorpio," I said as we both laughed.

We danced a lot that night. When it was near closing time, I was sitting down talking to my co-worker and Maynard walked into the club. Maynard spoke to me, spoke to Jordan, who was on the other side of the club with his friends, and then he walked back out of the front door. Jordan wanted to ride with me when I took my co-worker home so we just parked my car over at my mom's and took her home in his car. Then we picked my car up and went to my apartment. Jordan parked his car on the side street and I parked my car in front of my apartment. I was so happy because I was back with my honey and I was in my own place. We were laughing and having fun in each other's arms when the phone started ringing. I just let it ring but Maynard would only hang up and call right back. Finally in between calls I took the phone off the hook. Fifteen minutes later there was a knock at my door. Maynard was determined for me to get tired and just answer the door, but I wouldn't. Then the window on the door broke.

"Should I call the police?" I asked Jordan.

"Yeah, I guess", he said. "Damn, I wasn't finished yet. I wanted seconds. I guess you'd better bathe me first," he smiled as he kissed me again. I got my portable face bowl. With soap and warm water I gently bathed him as I did every time we made love. Then I called the police when we had finished. The police came and I opened the wooden door. I left the bars locked as I talked to the police.

"Do you want us to arrest him mam?" the police asked.

"Why don't you just go home, Maynard?" I pleaded.

"Why don't you let me in to see who's in there?" Maynard screamed.

"Why do you want to see who's in here?" I asked.

"Let me see who's in there," he screamed again.

"You know who's in here. Why don't you go home?" I asked.

"Mam, he's not going to calm down. You want us to arrest him?" the police asked again.

I started thinking about his mom having to bail him out and how long I had been friends with him and his family, before we decided to be more than just friends, so I mistakenly told them, "That's ok. Let him go." I really should have had him arrested, but I let him in to try to calm him down. Maynard started screaming at Jordan, picked up a bottle, broke it, and started towards Jordan. I stood in between them and said, "What are you doing? You've got to calm down. You know he can't go anywhere without protection." Jordan opened up his jacket to calmly show Maynard his shoulder holster, but didn't say a word.

"He's not going to just stand here and let you stab him with this bottle. Put it down," I said. Maynard put the bottle down and started shaking me.

"Why did you do this to me?" he had the audacity to say.

Jordan said as he headed for the door, "I'll talk to you later."

"OK", I said, wondering what the police were saying when they saw Jordan walk out. It took me about an hour to calm Maynard down. He finally left, threatening to hurt Jordan and everybody that Jordan knew. That's when I decided to take Maynard back just to keep the peace in the neighborhood, especially since Jordan called the next day to tell me that Maynard's brother said I was going to get him killed, and for him not to come back over. I do think that it was a mistake for me to let Maynard in, because what if I could not have controlled him; someone could have gotten hurt. Of course, Jordan mentioned that he'd been in a similar situation before. The girl who had lost his twins left the father of her two sons standing outside of their apartment, angry and banging on the door. I still felt that she had put Jordan in a more dangerous situation than I did, because she was still with her children's father. Maynard and I had broken up. Plus Jordan had been with many girls that had other boyfriends or husbands. I was in more danger being with him, than him being with me. But, it didn't matter. I had to humor Maynard before he caused any more problems, anyway.

"I know why you're letting me come over here everyday," Maynard said.

"Oh, really? Why do you think I'm letting you come over here every day?" I asked calmly.

He laughed and said, "Never mind."

"Yeah, never mind," I tried to say sweetly as I touched his shoulder, but I really wanted to wring his neck.

One of Maynard's friends was dating one of my friends and they came over one day with jokes.

"What are ya'll doing, taking turns getting caught?" We all laughed, but it wasn't really funny. I cared about Maynard and his family, but I had to call the landlord to have my window fixed, just because he was an egomaniac. He may have loved me, but he loved being a playboy more. He knew he pushed me back to Jordan, playing around with other women. One night Maynard and I were supposed to go out to a birthday party for a couple of our very close friends. Maynard took me to the club and left me. He said he had to go to his ex-girlfriend's grandmother's funeral. Now, maybe I should have been a little more understanding, but I thought that he should have sent a card, went and expressed his condolences earlier in the day, or just stopped by the funeral home and signed the book on the way to the party. No, he left the party, came back for a minute and then left again. Well, after he left the second time, in walked my Jordan.

"Where's your boyfriend?" he asked.

"He's at a funeral with his ex-girlfriend," I said.

"Good", he said as we started dancing. We danced, played around and had a good time. We were still on the dance floor when Maynard returned. All my friends were sitting at the table waving their hands and whistling trying to get my attention. I saw them, and I saw him. By then I didn't care.

"Tell him to go back to his ex where he came from," I said turning my back to them.

"Here comes Maynard", I told Jordan.

"Talk to you later", we both said as Maynard snatched me off the dance floor and began to drag me out of the club. I saw my friends just shaking their heads. We got in Maynard's car, left and he drove back around to the front of the club. He saw one of my friends from our table and told her, "Jan, go get Jordan and bring him outside. Tell him I want to talk to him," he said angrily.

I shook my head 'no' to her in a way that Maynard couldn't see, and she went in and never came back out. Maynard was pissed again.

"I guess I'm never supposed to speak to him ever again in my life," I pouted. "You were with your ex tonight, when you were supposed to be with me and our friends," I said.

This set me back another two weeks and I was getting tired of consoling Maynard and his BS. Plus, I missed my honey, even though until this party, I didn't think his family would let him come back to me after Maynard's drama. I really tried to love Maynard again, anyway, after that, but then he disappeared for a couple of days. I was at work depressed, wondering who he was with this time. He had as many women as Jordan, yet he just wasn't honest about them. All I could do to console myself was to say, "I usually get my man, but if I don't, maybe it's meant for me to get my sweet scorpion back."

I tried to convince myself to think positively of either outcome. I refused to allow myself to wallow too long in pain. Maynard showed up with some lame explanation that I didn't believe, but I accepted it because Jordan hadn't called me anyway.

A few weeks later, my sister asked me to come to California for Christmas. I put in for a 2-week vacation and started making my plans to go. Maynard was still coming over to my apartment everyday and occasionally we'd go to the movies or out to dinner. I stayed away from anywhere Jordan might be, just to keep the peace. I was hallucinating on the last work day before my vacation, so I couldn't go in to work. They thought I just wanted to catch an early plane, but I had sat in a 3-hour movie, drinking cough medicine trying to make my sore throat go away, and it caught up with me in the morning. My head would not stop spinning around. I had taken too much. I know now that I should have been drinking orange juice, but I got on the plane that night anyway.

I called Jordan after I was there a few days. I had an airline credit card to send for him, (although I knew he probably could pay for it himself). I didn't leave my sister's number with his mom, and for some reason I didn't try later. I was still sick with the flu. Plus, I guess I figured that by the time his mom found him, I'd probably be at home and back at work. Maynard, in the meantime, had resumed his life as a playboy. I guess all he needed was that break to remember that he wasn't ready to settle down with one girl. He was happy being free again, and I was happy for the both of us. I have to give him his props though. He was a very smart man and he should have been in college somewhere, while he was trying **not** to settle down with a wife. Even though he never stopped being a playboy, he did return and graduate from junior college; and he became a serious businessman who formed corporations and got grants to give Easter baskets to kids every year.

Sweet Scorpion
56

Chapter 3:
FREE, BUT CRAVING JORDAN

Now free, my friends and I went out stag as often as possible, but my mind was on Jordan, daily. I purposely tried to run into him whenever luck would let me. I let him know that I was free, but he had moved in with some other girl. That didn't last too long, because he started calling me 2 or 3 nights a week, and he said she had moved out of town. I'm not the type to chase a man or be too forward, but when I finally sat down with him, I had to let him know my dilemma.

"I think about you every night and every day. I can't help it. I think I'm addicted to you. I've been waiting for you to come back. I think I love you," I said.

"I know," he said. "I saw Nick at the club the other night. He told me he was trying to hit on you for himself, and he said all you kept saying was 'Have you seen Jordan around?' I know you miss me baby," he said, and then he kissed me.

Jordan began coming over only a couple a nights a week for a while, torturing me with his absence. "Can't I just come over here to sleep sometimes?" he said one night.

"Do I always have to --- umh --- ok?"

He always called me first to ask me if he could come over, I guess out of courtesy, and to keep from making the trip for nothing. One night he called and I had a friend over.

"Can I come over tonight?" he asked. The phone was right next to my friend and I guess I wasn't thinking fast enough. I wanted to say "Give me half an hour then you can come over", but I just said "No, not tonight." When I hung up, my heart sank. I didn't want to say no. My friend left right after that and I spent the rest of the night wondering, "What was I thinking?" The following afternoon the doorbell rang. It was Jordan.

"What? Did you have some man over here last night?" he asked. Before I could answer he said, "Give me those door keys." He snatched them from me and went to his car to get his TV and some of his clothes. I was so happy. I could have cried. I was thinking, I should have said "no" weeks ago. That's all I wanted was for him to be with me everyday, living with me. I was happy now.

One afternoon Jordan came home from the barbershop and told me, "I saw Maynard at the barbershop. I talked to him for a while. I reminded him that you were mine in the first place; and that you wouldn't have even been with him if I wasn't messing up."

"What did he say to that?" I asked.

"He agreed. We're cool now," he said.

"That's good," I said.

After Jordan was there for a few weeks, I asked about a concert that was coming to town. My friends and I never missed a concert and he and his friends didn't either.

"Can we go together this time?" I asked.

"I'm sorry baby, I already have plans. I already promised someone that I'd take them," he said, sounding really sorry.

"Who is it?" I asked.

"I can't tell anybody," he said. "It's a secret."

I figured it must have been some married woman, so I didn't ask any more questions, but he told me to stay at home. He had just moved in and I guess he really didn't want me to see him with her, whoever she was. But my friends and I never missed a concert; and I wasn't about to start missing any. "Obeying" wasn't in my vocabulary yet. So, I went to the concert, as usual, and I did look around to see if I could find him, but I couldn't. Usually after concerts, people go to the club. And since I knew Jordan had gone out, I thought he might have done the same thing. I don't know what I was thinking. It didn't even cross my mind that he would be with someone, if I did find him. I just went clubbing with all my friends trying to find him. (Of course I didn't tell my friends why I was going along.) The night was totally sad for me because I couldn't find him out that night. When I got home feeling hurt and sad, to my surprise, he was there in bed. I was so happy, and mad at myself for not coming straight home.

"Didn't I tell you not to go out tonight? You're too hip," he said, as I jumped into bed and tried to snuggle up next to him.

"Don't touch me," he said, as he turned his back to me, and went to sleep. Now my mind was all messed up. I quit going out and was there any time he needed me. I was now the dutiful, obedient, Suzy-homemaker-like wife, I was raised to be. I still didn't miss any concerts though, that was too much to ask of me, and so he didn't request that anymore. I know now that I should have continued to show up at the clubs he frequented instead of staying in, waiting for him to come home, because sometimes he didn't come home. He went home with whoever showed up at the club instead of me. He knew he had me totally under control after a while, and he would even send me home from parties, completely taking me for granted.

"Is there just one girl out there that you're with when you don't come home, or is there still a lot of them?" I asked, thinking if there's a lot, I may continue to take my chances with him. But if there's one girl out there that had his heart and attention, I couldn't continue to sit around accepting this foolishness.

"I have a lot of girls, you know that. Why?" he asked with genuine interest.

"We don't get intimate that much anymore and I want to go out with you sometimes. I want to go to parties, out to dinner, and to the movies, sometimes. And I want to go with you," I whined.

"Ah baby. You're my wife. All the girls wish they had your position. And as far as the sex, you know wives don't get none, only the mistresses," he laughed.

I didn't think that was very fair or funny. One evening he called me at work and told me to come straight home because one of our friends was having a party that night. His car was in the shop and he was too tired to get up and take me to work that day. He normally would have already left without me. We got to the party and his body guard and best friend Jeremy, who rode with us, decided he wanted to stick his protection into my purse. The protection went off. Everybody screamed and ran out of the party. Now there was a hole in my new purse. The owner calmed the crowd down and everybody came back in, not knowing what happened, but they knew there were no fights or anything, so they stayed. I told Jordan what happened and he got pissed.

"Don't get mad at him," I said, feeling sorry for Jeremy. Sometimes he did act like Barney Fife; even though he was sincere about not letting anybody hurt Jordan or me. Now, Jordan was mad at me too, for taking up for him. He told Jeremy to take me home, and come back. On the way home I said,

"Why does he always send me home? Today is my birthday," I whined.

"It's getting kind of dangerous out here these days. We can hardly go to the clubs or anywhere without somebody trying to start something. These people shoot at folks, you know. Did you tell him it was your birthday?" he asked.

"No," I said.

"Well, how was he going to know?"

Jeremy checked my apartment thoroughly, in the closet and in the bathroom. "You're secure. Lock the door behind me."

About a half hour later, I heard Jordan coming in the door.

"Why didn't you tell me it was your birthday baby," he asked.

"I don't know," I said, knowing that I'd never been the type that asked anybody for anything. So I just didn't say anything.

"You're nuts", he said as he kissed me, and we spent the rest of the night, my birthday, together. When we woke in the morning I decided that when Jordan's birthday came, I would surprise him with something nice.

"When is your birthday?" I asked.

"In October. I was born the day before my mother's birthday. I was a sweet present for her, wasn't I?" he asked jokingly.

"A 'sweet scorpion', huh?" I joked back.

"Yep, a sweet scorpion for Elizabeth," he said.

"Your mom's name is Elizabeth? My middle name is Elizabeth," I said.

"See, I'm Elizabeth's 'Sweet Scorpion'," he said, kissing me for more. Things were better then.

"Who is that soft-talking person that answers your home phone," my most inquisitive friend asked.

"That's Jordan," I told her.

"The Jordan?" she questioned, knowing we actually had three Jordan's that closely ran around with us. The other two were boyfriends of our close friends. They use to hang out at my place a lot too.

"Hum. Homeboy done moved in huh?"

"Yeah, but I don't tell everybody that."

"I gotcha........."

Jordan was very popular with the ladies at the colleges where she and all my friends attended school. Every time she heard anything about him she would call me and report. She called once saying, "There was a girl in the ladies' lounge at school saying she was Jordan's girlfriend and he wanted her to look for an apartment for them to live in," she said.

"What?" I asked. "Who is she? What did she look like?" I was thinking, but she was volunteering that information before I could ask.

"Her name is Tiffany. She's short. She wears a maroon leather jacket like yours. She's cute most of the time, you know, we all have good days and bad days," she said.

"He usually tells me everything. We'll see," I said. When I hung up, I was very nervous and sad. "I hope this isn't one of those days that he stays gone all day," I thought. He came in about an hour later and I immediately confronted him.

"I got a phone call telling me there was a girl named Tiffany in the student lounge saying she was your girlfriend and that you guys were looking for an apartment together. Is that true?"

"What? This girl ...is telling people my business. Naw, it's not true. I'm not moving anywhere with her. I'll be right back," he said, pretty pissed. I was sure he went to quit her, but every day when I came home from work, the first thing I did was check to make sure his things were still there. A few months later her name came up again because she was now telling him she was pregnant. But the same day he told me this, he also told me and several of his friends that were with us, that three other girls were also claiming to be pregnant too. They all started laughing and he started laughing too. The first thing I said was "You can't be getting all these girls pregnant. What are you going to do with all these kids?"

"You sound just like my sister," he said. "I just came from my sister's house. She just said the same thing you did," he said.

"Well, I don't think it's funny, because I'm pregnant too," I said, trying not to laugh. Everybody turned and looked at me. I think they all were waiting for me to start laughing, so I held it for a while, a long while, but we all started laughing anyway. I wasn't really, but I must admit I wished I was. I even went to a doctor to see what was wrong with me.

What was the reason why I couldn't get pregnant, other than he was too busy sleeping with everybody but me?

"Don't worry. They can't all be pregnant by me. I don't see most of them but once a month. I know they have other men. I know a few of their old secrets. They ain't fooling me," he said.

Fortunately only two were really pregnant, but that was two too many. According to him, he gave one of them money to eliminate the problem, but she showed up at his best friend's house two months later with a belly, saying she couldn't do it. They both were very nice and sweet girls. His daughter's mother went to my church, and he said she was just like me. I had seen and met her before I met him, so I knew she was a very pretty girl. To see where his head was, I asked, "Why don't you marry Cindy? She's very nice and very pretty."

"She went back to her husband because I hadn't been over there in a couple of months," he said.

I guess she saw that he was not going to commit, and if she was really like me, already having one child, she got scared that she would be a single mother of two. She and her husband decided not to tell anyone there was another father involved. I was glad to hear that Jordan wasn't thinking of marrying her. I didn't really want him to marry anybody but me. He said she made a familiar comment.

"You bugged me for four years and I wouldn't leave Mark. The fifth year, after I get married, have a baby, and my husband acts up, I finally give in to you, now you're no longer interested. This is my baby. I'll take care of it myself." She did call his mom from the hospital though, to let them know that the baby was born. It was a little girl and it arrived two months before his son did.

"I want to start bank accounts for both of them. Maybe I can start them at $5,000 a piece and let their mothers build them from there, if I don't get back around to adding to them. What do you think?" he asked.

"Sounds good to me," I said.

My number one spy Operetta called again. "Marisa just got beat up by her boyfriend for being with your man? She's at school with sunglasses on, hiding her black and blues," she said. "She supposedly already told Jordan she was going to stay with her man, because she couldn't deal with all of Jordan's women. She still does all the alterations on his clothes though.

"I guess her man doesn't want her to have any 'friends', you think?" I said.

"No. I guess not," Operetta said.

One night Jordan and Jeremy picked me up from work in Jeremy's car. As we approached my front porch, my new neighbor was moving in the last of her things.

"What's up? It's you that's moving in upstairs?" Jeremy asked.

"Yes," she said.

"This is Jordan and Erin. They live downstairs under you," he said as he turned to us.

"Jordan, Erin, this is Cecelia."

"Hi, Cecelia. Welcome to the neighborhood," I said.

"Nice to meet you," Jordan said.

We all talked for a while, then Jordan and I went in to get ready for bed. Jeremy went upstairs with Cecelia. We were lying in the bed watching television when I heard two big thumps. I started laughing. Jordan looked at me strangely because he wasn't paying attention, so he hadn't caught on.

"Jeremy just dropped his boots to let us know he was getting him some," I laughed.

"Wha-a-t?" he laughed, shaking his head.

"You guys know every girl in this city, don't you?" I asked Jeremy, when he came downstairs the next morning.

"Just about," he said smiling.

Many nights I sat at home alone longing for Jordan and wishing he had waited for me to get off work before he went out. I finally I decided to start going out, in hopes of running into him. When I got home between 1:15 A.M. and 1:30 A.M., I would always sit in my pretty dresses hoping he would come home and see me all dressed before I went to bed. I wanted him to remember that what he had at home could look just as pretty as what he found out in the clubs. Three o'clock would always roll around and I would give up and get ready for bed. Every time I would give up, take off my clothes and go to bed, he would walk in the door.

"Hi, babe. I'm hungry. How about some breakfast? Eggs, biscuits, applesauce, sausage, and rice; you know, the works," he'd say.

"OK", I'd say and not even cook anything for myself when I started breakfast. Still trying to get more time with Jordan, I asked for the vacancy on the day shift. I wanted to be available when he got ready to go out, because by the time I got off at 11:00 P.M., he was already gone. Standing up against the wall in a deep sleep at work, I felt a tap on my shoulder, "Erin, are you going out tonight?" my friend Louise asked.

"I don't know," I yawned, realizing that I should have stayed on the evening shift. "I have to see what Jordan's going to do. I'll call you," I said, wishing I was in bed asleep. He always kept me up all night talking, laughing, or cooking.

When I got home from work, I laid down for a while. Jordan and Jeremy showed up surprisingly about 10:00 P.M., which was early for them. Jordan got on the phone and after talking a few minutes, I heard him say "Damn, she hung up on me," and he redialed her.

"Don't hang up on me. Let me talk to you," he said. She hung up again and he redialed her again.

"Look baby. Let me talk to you. Uh – wait – damn," he said as he redialed again.

"Who is he talking to?" I finally asked Jeremy.

"Paula," Jeremy said, as if he was wondering when I was going to say something.

"Jordan man, forget Paula. Erin's here and will always be here. Forget that one," he said in my behalf.

But Paula kept milking it for all it was worth. She was finally getting a rise out of him to act like he cared, so she kept hanging up. I got my work clothes ready for the next morning, and said, "I'll see you later."

"Where are you going?" Jordan asked.

"Out," I said and went straight to Louise's to spend the night. I was hoping that he thought I went with some man because I wanted a caring response, but he said the next day that he knew I was with Louise. "You ride to work with her every morning, don't you?" he said, confidently, still not paying me any attention. I can't help but wonder why Jordan picked that night to be on the phone with Paula. It was a few days after Jordan's brother Rick had come over for dinner and spent some time with us. We played cards and had fun all night and I felt very comfortable with Jordan's family around, but I wasn't going to get pushy like Fontana. She felt she had an Ace card with Rick's wife, because she came into the family already having two kids also. Fontana even stated that Rick's wife was her Ace.

So she always remarked, "My big brother Rick this, and my big brother Rick that." She was really sickening. Rick's wife had two babies for Rick as soon as she entered the family. Fontana didn't, so there was a difference ("miscarriage" or not). Maybe Jordan didn't want me to think that he was choosing whoever was closest to his brother, after hearing her annoying mouth.

"Erin" was starting to look like a very popular or common name because Jordan's two best and closest friends/body guards and his only brother and him, all had girlfriends named Erin. Jordan's worst enemy's wife was named Erin too.

"All you Erin's are something else," Jordan said, one day as we were just lying around relaxing.

"What are you talking about?" I asked.

"One day, my brother walked into the store where my friend Billy's girlfriend works. They started flirting with each other. So his Erin is the same girl as Billy's Erin. I'm in the middle of it, and I know one day it's going to hit the fan," he said. "My brother has a girlfriend at home too, and one of her friends made an "I should tell" remark to Erin; and Billy's friends said they are starting to feel disloyal because he's looking like a fool, since he's the only other one who doesn't know what's going on," Jordan said, shaking his head. Two days later, Billy's friends said they couldn't stand it any longer and my phone rang.

"Jordan," Billy said, "Meet me at Erin's mother's house. I just got told about your brother. I know you couldn't tell me, but I can't handle this. Go with me when I talk to her."

"OK," Jordan said looking at me and holding his head. "Damn. Billy's mess just hit the fan. I knew this was going to happen. I was Erin's friend before I was his. I met him through her, and Rick is my brother," he said hurrying out of the door. "Let me go get him. I'll be back," he said as he ran to the car. Forty-five minutes later, Jordan showed up with Erin.

"Hi. So you're the other Erin." "We've known each other since high school," she told Jordan.

Jordan went to the bedroom. He had left Billy to go think, by himself and brought Erin to chill with us. "I feel bad," she told me, "but when he had a baby with another girl, I couldn't handle it," she said.

"I understand," I said.

"You knew about that girl?" she asked.

"Yeah, I knew, and I totally understand," I said.

She continued anyway. "I couldn't handle him getting some other girl pregnant in the middle of our relationship. Rick came along and relieved my pain."

"I know," I said.

"Billy just came over there upset and wanted me to go downstairs to the basement so we could talk it over; and my mom stepped in front of me and said 'if you want to talk to her, talk right up here.' My mom's my girl. She had to protect herself from my dad once, so she knew he was too mad to leave him to be alone with me," she said as she started to calm down.

Later, Jordan and I took her home and then he called his brother. "Rick man, he knows. He doesn't want any static, because you're my brother, but he's devastated."

"Man it was an accident. She started kinda flirting with me a little at the store and we let vibes carry us the rest of the way, and she "is fine," Jordan told me his brother said.

"Yeah, and she didn't enter a relationship with Billy like me and you. They had a one-on-one relationship, so when he got Angie pregnant, she couldn't handle it," he said. "I'm actually relieved. I was tired of holding that secret. I knew it was going to get out eventually and like I said, I was her friend first. His new daughter is a pretty little girl, too. Erin was really upset about that."

A few days later, Jordan said, "Billy married Erin on the promise that she would break off the relationship with Rick."

"That's good," I said.

"Good? I wouldn't have married her, I would have..."

"You would have what? I thought she was your friend first?" I asked.

"She is my friend, but she still needs a spanking; plus, I think she still loves my brother," he laughed.

"Yeah, well. She got what she wanted all along. I'm glad for her. She just wanted him to marry her. It's good she could bounce back," I said, remembering how I couldn't return to Angelo after being with Jordan. Our vibes were gone.

"You know, she actually said 'I got him now,'" he said.

"Good," I said.

"Yeah, we'll see," Jordan said.

Chapter 4:
THE CITY'S GETTING "HOT"

The city was starting to get really dangerous. It was the early to mid-seventies. The Vietnam conflict had ended and everyone was home from that awful war. The "free love and drugs" era came home with the troops at the war's ending. Everybody was just happy at first, but then the atmosphere changed with bootlegging-type drug wars.

"You may catch a stray bullet if you just happened to be at the wrong place at the wrong time. You could be at the grocery store, or just walking down the street to a neighbor's," Billy's Erin said one day when we were all sitting around.

"And you aren't making it easier for any of us to go out anywhere, when you let all those wives cry on your shoulder every time their husbands do something stupid," I said to Jordan.

"I know. I don't tell anybody I even know none of ya'll at all. Ya'll got half the city wanting one of those stray bullets to find ya'll," Erin said, as we all laughed.

The phone rang on Saturday morning.

"Hello," I said.

"Hey, Erin. Whatcha doing?" my sister Charmayne asked.

"Nothing. Now that I'm on days, I have most weekends off. I was relaxing. Why? Are you here in town?" I asked.

"Yes. I'll be right over," she said. The doorbell rang and I opened it.

"Hi. Come on and ride with me," she said after she hugged me.

"Let's go to Les Ami for lunch. They're supposed to have good food," she said assuredly. "When are you coming to California to live?" she asked, as we were being seated in Les Ami's.

"You keep saying that maybe you'll make your move next month, but next month never happens."

"I know. I'm just not ready to leave yet; and Jordan is not ready for me to leave either," I said, wishing that he was dining with us. It was starting to bother me that we could never go out to the movies, dinner, or anywhere to have fun.

"Jordan? That Jordan sounds like a jet-setter to me. You must be his mother image. Is he really your type, or vice-versa?" she asked.

"I'm home to him," I said, trying to understand what 'mother-image' meant.

"Yeah, mother image, like I said," she piped in.

"I'm the wife he comes home to. Men usually marry women who make them feel comfortable like their mother, sister, or family does --- his mother image --- well, I guess that might be it," I thought.

"That was a pretty nice lunch," Charmayne said as we left. We paid our tab, headed for the door and drove to a friend's house.

"Hey. How are you doing? You know my sister Erin, don't you?" my sister gestured to me as we entered her friend's house.

"This is Doc and his wife Eva," Charmayne said.

"Hi. Nice to meet you," I said.

"Same here," Doc and Eva both responded.

"We just checked out that new restaurant you guys told me about," continued Charmayne. "It was pretty decent. Erin lives right down the street from there," Charmayne said to Doc.

"Have you talked to your sister today?" Doc asked Eva. "She was supposed to have a party sometime this week, if you're still here," he said to Charmayne.

"Thanks for the invite," replied Charmayne.

"No, come to think of it I have not," Eva responded, after thinking about the question. "Her husband was probably too pissed off. He's crazy enough to say he's going to shoot Jordan, right in the courtroom on the day his liquor licensing is scheduled. Some 'friends of his' told him that they saw his name on the docket; so he's going into a building full of police and judges, shooting people," she said shaking her head in disgust. "I'll call her later when I think he's in a better mood. She shouldn't have gone back to that 'ignant man'," she snarled.

"Jordan?" I'm thinking to myself. "At least these people don't have a clue who I am. I've got to warn him," I thought.

When I got back home, Jordan wasn't there, so I plopped down on the bed to sleep off the buzz I got from some new drink my sister ordered for me - A King Alphonse Tall, or something.

The next day as we entered the courtroom and sat down, I saw a man come from behind one of the pillars. Before I could get Jordan's complete attention, bullets were ringing out and I dropped to the floor behind the bench in front of us. The gun had stopped firing but Jordan and his brother were lying next to me covered in blood. My heart sank as I leaned over to see if they were still alive. I wiped Jordan's forehead and took a quick look around to make sure no other bullets would come in our direction, as I heard security chasing suspects down the hall. I put my hands on Jordan's chest to begin CPR, but for some reason I just wanted to kiss him first. I pressed on his heart intentionally as I leaned forward to kiss his lips and...

I sat up in bed real fast in a cold sweat. I was dreaming. I had fallen asleep without trying to find him, to warn him. "There's no court date tonight," I said to myself, "but I'd better try to find him anyway." I called Billy's house.

"Hey, Erin. Is Jordan over there?" I asked.

"No. He did call earlier though, but he hasn't been here," she said.

"If he calls, tell him to call home," I said.

"OK," she said.

"Hello," Jeremy's Erin said, when she answered the phone.

"Hi Erin," I said. "Is Jordan there?"

"No, he and Jeremy left about an hour ago."

"If he comes back through there, please tell him to call home," I said, worrying about them riding around in the streets. Of course, I tried to stay up half the night to wait for Jordan to come home, but this was the one night he didn't show until mid-morning the next day.

"I've been calling around looking for you," I said to him as he entered the bedroom.

"What's up? Did you need me for something baby?" he said smiling in his BS voice.

"I was over someone's house yesterday who claims to know your court date. The guy said one of your girlfriend's husband would catch you off guard there, and shoot you." I was very upset that he was just getting home. I was more upset that I worried about him more than he worried about himself.

"Nobody's crazy enough to shoot up a courtroom," he said nonchalantly.

"Okay, whatever. I'm just telling you what I heard," I said, surprised that he seemed unconcerned.

"Thanks for looking out, baby, but I'm not going to worry about it," he said as he lay down on the bed. I lay beside him and tried to forget about the warning.

I must have fallen asleep again because I suddenly saw tall, golden brown and handsome Jordan walking through the airport doors with his folded garment bag over his shoulders and his matching luggage in his hands.

"Hi baby. You're looking real cute today. Did you use the grocery money I gave you to buy this new outfit?" he said, *pulling on the tube top I had on under my jean suit.*

"No," I said. *"I have my own money, you know that."*

"Yeah, right. Every time I leave some money with a woman to keep for me, they spend it," he said *teasingly.*

"You told me to buy groceries and things for the apartment. That's what I did with 'your' money," I said.

"Unh hunh, right. We'll see," he said.

Suddenly, I felt someone shaking me. Drudgingly, I opened my eyes, thinking "Why am I constantly having these weird dreams? Is Jordan trying to think of excuses to leave me?"

"Have you heard from Billy and Erin?" Jordan asked.

"Yeah. We all went to see the O'Jays and Chaka Kahn last night," I said.

"Really? How was it?" he asked, sorry he missed the show.

"It was real nice, and one of the O'Jays was out sick; but they put on a real nice show anyway," I said, wishing he had been with us, especially when they sang "Let Me Make Love To You." I craved for Jordan every time I heard that song. Later that day we visited Billy and Erin.

"Hey. What's up? Come on in and have a seat," Billy said as he showed us to the living room.

"Hi," Erin said, "nice suit."

"Yeah. I know she bought that with my money," Jordan said.

"Give it a rest. I bought this with my own money. I do have a job," I said, hurt for real, because I've always been the one he could trust.

"You know she won't spend your money man. I tried to get her to go in your money when we ran out of V.O. and wine at the club, but she said she won't touch anything without your approval, and we couldn't find you. I had to respect that. We should get some though, first thing in the morning," Billy said.

"You could have given him the money for that," Jordan looked at me and said.

"Don't worry about it. She did right, if you didn't approve it first. They had enough for last night," Billy said.

"You missed Chaka Kahn last night man. That red headed beauty is my woman." Billy glanced at Erin to see if she would react.

"It was a nice show, and she can play the heck out of some drums," Erin said, giving him the reaction he expected or wanted, by rolling her eyes at him.

"That's my girl too. She's a bad gal," Jordan said.

"The O'Jays put on a hell of a show too, and it was only two of them," Billy said.

"Yeah, it didn't take away from the show at all," I added.

"Unh, unh," Erin agreed.

"I'm tired man. We're sleeping over here tonight, okay. I'll call Jeremy and let him know when to come and get us. I've got to get up early and meet my brother in court," Jordan said.

"You know where the bedroom is. See you in the morning," Billy said.

"What-cha been doing while I was gone, looking all sexy," Jordan asked, pulling on my tube top as usual, this time pulling it off my breast.

"Those torpedoes still there, I see?" he said kissing them, making me forget all the pain he had put me through. That night went well.

As I stepped out of the shower in the morning, Erin pointed and said, "There's some bacon, eggs, and biscuits here in the 'fridge. I'll put them on the counter for you. I've got to go to my mother's house. So I'll see you guys later. I'll meet you in the courtroom," she whispered, not wanting Billy to know that she would even be in the same building with Rick, Jordan's brother, even if it was just for moral support.

I commenced to cooking breakfast for all the guys, including Jeremy, who showed up early to wake us up for court. I was used to cooking for them at my house, but I couldn't help thinking that Erin had done left me to mammy-maid them, all by myself. She didn't know that all the girls envied her because Billy didn't allow her to work and he just showered her with cars, clothes, expensive hairstyles, and jewelry, while the rest of us went to work everyday and didn't have nothin'. I loved her though. She was pretty cool.

Jeremy drove us to the courthouse, of course with his protection strapped to his side. We pulled up to a building that looked like a church. We got out of the car, and went in to find a seat. I was remembering, as I entered the building, that this was the day that was supposed to end in gunfire, according to my dream. So I started looking around the room in every nook and cranny. During the whole court procedure, I kept scanning the room and the doorways. Luckily there was no one else that I knew in the courtroom. It appeared to be nobody but club owners in the whole little building. I still thought it was a church, but maybe not. Anyway, the Lord must have been there somewhere, because nothing happened and the liquor license was cleared, for Rick and Jordan. Luckily Erin didn't show up and neither did Billy.

Jordan let me hang out with him at Billy's all day. For two more days we just visited other friends. I called in sick so I would not miss the opportunity. Maybe it would have lasted longer, but I figured I'd better say something about going home to change clothes before he did. Sure, we bathed at other peoples' houses, but I had to put back on the same clothes. He, of course, had clothes at everybody's place. I didn't want to end the two-day buddy-buddy relationship, but I took a chance on him saying he would go home with me and wait for me to change. He didn't.

As I was getting ready to try to find Jordan the next day, the phone rang and it was Nan and Karla, two friends of his who asked if I wanted to go to lunch with them.

"Hey Karla," I said, as I entered Nan's house the next day.

"Hi Erin," she said, extra happy to see me for some reason.

"I'm glad you came," she said. "I need to talk to you. You know I left your man's buddy, Leonard, don't you?"

"Yeah, Jordan told me," I replied.

"He just, I don't know, turned me off. He acted like he was never going to grow up and be his own man, so I found me somebody else," she continued.

"There's not a problem is there?" I questioned.

"The problem is, the 'somebody else' is Craig's cousin Donald, another one of Jordan's worst enemies," she said.

"What?" I acted horrified and thinking, "This town is getting too small."

"Yeah, but I just found out last night that Donald and Craig are cousins. I don't want them and Jordan to have a shoot out with me in the middle, since I'm Jordan's friend."

"I know what you mean," I replied.

"But maybe it's a good thing because, since Craig's wife went back to him and stopped fooling around with Jordan, maybe I can get them to calm down and stop being so hostile towards Jordan. And that will be good for you too."

"You're right about that," I said.

"Do you think Jordan would come to a meeting at Donald's club, if Craig will agree to it?" she pleaded sincerely.

"I don't know. I'll ask him. He surely doesn't want people shooting at him all of the time, so he might agree," I added.

"In the meantime, tell him if he sees a white flag waving when Craig is shooting at him, it's me, and be careful not to hit me if he shoots back," she said. Then we all started laughing.

After we had lunch, I went home thinking, "If I arrange this meeting and that clown shoots my man anyway, Jordan will think I set him up. I don't know about this, but I may decide to tell him what she said anyway."

"No, baby," Jordan responded. "I don't trust him. He might say he's going to behave, just to get me there. Hunh … she said she's going to wave a white flag? She's so silly," he said laughing.

My phone rang the next afternoon. "Hello. Is Jordan there?" the voice asked.

"No he isn't. Who's calling?" I asked.

"This is Fontana. Is this his sister?" she asked.

"No," I said.

"Is this Myrtle? (his brother's 1st wife)," she asked.

"Is this his mother?" she kept asking.

"No. This is Erin," I finally said, actually hesitating, because I knew I was busting him out and maybe hurting her feelings, crazily not thinking about my own feelings.

"Oh. This boy won't ever quit. Tell him I called," she said, and hung up. I already knew who the infamous Fontana was. She was the girl who cussed Judy out and the first girl to get pregnant by Jordan. She already had two sons and almost died when she had a miscarriage with Jordan's twins. She had decided not to leave the two boy's father anyway, but later changed her mind and longed for Jordan and the twins. I think when Judy called her nicely asking if she was still seeing Jordan, her ego was triggered and she started declaring her love for Jordan from long distance. He, unfortunately, gave her respect anyway, anytime she came to town. Whether it was due or not is a matter of opinion. I never bad-mouthed her or any of the girls though. I felt that if I couldn't win him on my own merits, without discrediting one of them, I wasn't supposed to have him. This particular girl was mean though, and I didn't really care for her. I didn't maliciously say anything to him about her though. Besides he praised everything she said and did, even if everybody else thought it was evil or ignorant. I wondered if she was too old for him though, since she called him a boy.

"You had a phone call," I hesitatingly said.

"Who was it?" he asked.

"It was Fontana," I said, wondering if I should have even told him.

"Did she leave a number?" he asked.

"No. She just wanted me to tell you that she called," I said.

"Her in-laws must have brought her here and put her in an apartment without a phone, so she won't call me like she always does," he said.

"They found out about me when her two son's father caught me in their apartment after he came home from the military. They don't like me for obvious reasons; and then the baby thing happened too. Oh well," he shrugged.

Later, one day I decided to do a thorough house-cleaning, which included going through his things. I found the first of a number of letters she sent, saying she enjoyed the time she spent with Jordan, his brother, and his brother's fiancée. She continued on about how good their four children played with her two children. She went on and on about them having so much in common; and kept referring to Jordan's brother as her brother-in-law. Jordan later told me that she sent letters, and left notes around on purpose to make her presence known and to make the other women jealous. I'm no longer going to worry about Fontana because she sounds just as insecure as the rest of us. I decided though that I was not going to stand for being neglected anymore. To my pain and surprise though, Jordan just left without saying anything. Jordan was gone for a couple of weeks and everyday when I came home; the first thing I'd do was make sure his TV and clothes were still there.

Two weeks was too long for me to sit around wondering about him. I also was wondering if I was being a darn fool letting him keep my keys, coming and going as he saw fit, and keeping me on hold. So I decided I'd better put my foot down and put his TV and things by the front door, indicating "get out".

A few more days went by and Jordan showed up on my day off. He opened the door, saw his things, and laughed harder than I ever heard him laugh.

"I guess I'm supposed to be put out?" he said. "You know you'd go crazy if you came home and didn't see my things still here," he said as if he could read my mind, and kept laughing. "Come on and ride with me," he said.

We went around to all of our friend's houses, just so he could tell them that I called myself putting him out. He still kept laughing. We all laughed, especially when he hugged me saying "You know you don't want me to really go anywhere, do you baby?" Later, he pushed me into one of Jeremy's spare bedrooms to make sure I wasn't serious about putting him out ... and I wasn't.

After that, in spite of my pouting, Jordan still decided to take a vacation to where Fontana lived. I got depressed while he was gone and in my heart, I started to feel for Bob, my high school first love. I called his mother to ask how she and he were doing. She told me he was on his way home, without his wife, because they were separated. He arrived the next morning and we spent the next four days together. I was still depressed and so was he. His wife had run off to New York and he was very hurt. Neither of us could camouflage our pain very well, but we tried to pretend we were enjoying ourselves. We even went to see Richard Pryor in concert where we ran into Billy and Erin.

I'm not sure they saw Bob though. If they did, they didn't say anything to me or Jordan. All Billy ever said was how pretty I looked. I had on one of my new dresses, hat, and shoes that I wanted Jordan to see me in, but I don't think he ever did. Bob went back to DC to try to get his wife back. A few days later, Jordan came home. I was very unhappy and I was starting to think it was time for me to move out of town with my sister, especially since I went all by myself to see "Alice Doesn't Live Here Anymore", at the movies. Also, Jordan brother's best friend had just gotten shot in the movie theater. So I guess I should have quit complaining about him not taking me out. I should have been leaving before my luck ran out anyway. People were starting to associate and recognize my car with Jordan and his friends. I didn't want people to start shooting at it. His car already had a million bullet holes in it.

After being gone again for about a week, Jordan came in talking to me as if I was his best friend. "Erin. I met a girl. She's half Puerto Rican and half black. She's real young and she's so sweet and I have had to teach her everything. I think I love her," he said seriously.

"Really?," I said, hurt but feeling a little relieved that maybe this foolishness will now end. He made a few phone calls and left with a totally different attitude.

"Oh well," I thought to myself, "why didn't I make him take his things and leave my keys?"

Two weeks later Jordan opened the door with his keys as usual as if he hadn't been anywhere. "What are you doing here? I thought you were in love?" I said, faking like I didn't care.

"I gave that broad my money to put in the bank for me and she spent it all. Plus, she wouldn't let any of my gals call my brother's place for me. I sent her back to Memphis," he said, like he was genuinely annoyed. He took a shower, turned on the TV, got in the bed and went to sleep. Home again, I guess.

Jordan's brother, Rick, decided to move his now wife and children out west so that she could go to school there with her sister. Instead of closing out his apartment, he let Jordan have it. I wanted us to move west with my sister also, or I wanted to move in with Jordan here. Jordan wasn't having either. He said he wanted to be a bachelor for a while. Consequently, I moved back to my moms' hesitatingly to get ready to leave the state without him. Jordan would only call me once every other week while I was at work to tell me he needed my car. I would always let him trade cars with me or take my car and come back to pick me up. He hadn't been around for a while and the last time, I had to catch a cab to and from work because he took the car and didn't bring it back. So I finally said, "No, you can't use my car." I said it trying to be strong, but hurting from wanting to see him.

"Yeah, okay," he said with an attitude.

That evening, he and Jeremy showed up at my job when I was getting ready to go home. He jumped into the driver's seat and we followed Jeremy to his place. "Jeremy, can you believe she told me I can't take the car?" Jordan said sarcastically, as he pushed me into Jeremy's spare room. He started taking off my clothes immediately. As usual, I started smiling.

"Unh huh. You'll say 'yes' to me knocking some off, but 'no' to me using the car," he said.

"You only call, every now and then, and it's to use the car. Why do you always call **me**, anyway?" I asked.

"Because you're dependable," he said.

"I want you to call for reasons other than I'm dependable," I whined.

"Ah, you miss me baby?" he said as he started kissing me all over my chest and undulating on my pelvis, but wouldn't get completely undressed.

"I know you're not going to throw away your underwear today?" I said.

"You don't deserve all – of -me - today," he said, as he groaned.

"I'll never have his baby like this," I thought to myself.

Jordan started calling me every night after that, asking me to meet him at his apartment anywhere from 2:00 A.M. to 4:00 A.M. in the morning. The calls suddenly stopped coming though, but I foolishly sat at home every night anyway waiting ... waiting ... waiting. After a month I decided that I must have been nuts and foolish. So I decided that I was going out and find me a real boyfriend. I had to get off the merry-go-round. I got dressed and went to the new supper club. I wasn't there five minutes when I was approached by a nice looking businessman and buyer for a popular shoe store in the area.

His name was Wesley. I was very impressed with him and I even liked his honest and down to earth conversation. Wesley and I went to the movies, out to dinner, and to his own arcade to play games. We went somewhere almost every night. Twice one of Jordan's buddy's girl-friend saw me out having dinner with Wesley. She said nothing because she wasn't with who she was supposed to be with either. All the guys did whatever they wanted to, but expected us to sit around alone (for weeks in Jordan's case), waiting on them.

One day when Wesley and I drove up in front of my mom's house, Jordan and Jeremy pulled up behind us as Wesley pulled off.

"You looking all cute. You don't wear braless halters with me," he said, pulling on my clothes as usual.

"You never take me out," I laughed. "Where have you been, anyway?" I asked.

"You're just trying to make me laugh so I won't clock you," he laughed, as he faked a punch at me.

"That's right, and where have you been?" I laughed.

"I've been busy, but I'm going to call you when I get back. I'm going to the concert in Atlanta," he said.

"I want to go," I said. Jordan just smiled.

"My friends are broke and I don't want to pay anybody's way. At the same time, I don't want to go by myself."

Can I go with you?" I whined.

"No. It's just the fellows this time," he said. "Maybe next time baby," he said. He got back in the car, and left.

So, I continued to go out with Wesley. The Atlanta concert weekend came and went and I heard nothing from Jordan. I ached for him. The 4th of July came and Wesley and I went to my family's picnic on the family property in the country. My family, including my aunts and cousins, loved Wesley.

"Do you like him?" my auntie asked. "You can learn to like a square, monogamous, intelligent man, with his own money," she and my mom persisted. Unfortunately, I knew Jordan would be back, and I also knew that I loved him and would let him come back. Besides, I always followed my heart and vibes. Young and dumb, I guess. I've had tamer guys anyway and they cheated just like Jordan. Jordan just didn't lie about it.

"What do you want to do tonight?" Wesley asked.

"I want to go to the War and AWB concert," I said, knowing I would see Jordan there. When we got to the concert, I saw why I had not heard from Jordan in weeks. The half Puerto Rican girl who took all his money and blocked all his girlfriends from calling was with him and Erin. They were sitting three sections across from us. However I didn't notice them until I excused myself to the bathroom during intermission. I walked right into Jordan's arms.

"Look at you again. When did you get this outfit?" he said, playing with my breast on a sly.

"I miss you," I said.

"I miss you too. You'll see me soon," he said. "Who are you with, anyway?" he asked.

"My friends," I said, thinking he might believe me, since I always went to the concerts with a bunch of girls. When I got back to my seat, I saw Erin and Laurie. Eventually Jordan joined them. If he looked through the audience as I did, he probably saw me too, but he never said anything. Two days later he came back to me though. Again, I spent most nights at his apartment. I guess Laurie, the Puerto Rican girl, got sent back to Memphis again.

Jordan usually came home at 2:00 A.M. or 3:00 A.M. to talk to me all night, whether I had to work in the morning or not. He actually got upset when I took some cough syrup and was nodding off when he needed my conversation.

"I'm sick, you nut," I said.

"I need you to stay awake with me," he said. "You'd stay awake if I were trying to knock me off some," he grunted.

"You're selfish, but I'm awake. Talk," I said, trying to sit up and listen.

The next night Jordan was sleeping so hard he barely knew I was there. I happily showered and lay down to sleep. I slept good, dreaming of Jordan and me. I dreamed that we were on our honeymoon and had exhaustingly fallen asleep. I heard someone rattling the doorknob. Then they busted in the door with both of us in the nude. The sheets had fallen to the floor. I was scared and flushed with embarrassment because I couldn't cover myself up. Then, I woke up completely, in a cold sweat.

"Whoa! I'm glad I was only dreaming," I said, but I still heard a rattle at the door, for real this time.

"Jordan," I said, shaking him hard. "There's somebody trying to break in." Jordan didn't budge. The door opened downstairs and I got the pistol from under the pillow.

"Jordan," I screamed, and he grunted. "Shit. I don't know how this thing works," I said as I fiddled with the safety button.

"Boom. Boom. Boom. Boom." It worked and I was too scared to stop shooting. By this time Jordan was up.

"Who is that?" I screamed. I was shaking and crying as he tried to take the gun from me, but I was too scared to let go or take my eyes off the intruder. Eventually Jordan calmed me down and I did let go of the trigger. The police and coroner came.

While they were questioning me, one of Jordan's female groupies came running in screaming, "I tried to stop him, Jordan. He had followed me the other day when I came over here. Oh my God is he ...?" she cried as she looked at the body on the stairs. I looked at Jordan and he looked at me. I went to her and grabbed her hand, looking up at the police.

"We need your statement," the police said to her. He already had mine. I didn't know what to say to her. I thought I should try to comfort her, though I needed comforting myself. Her brother, who had brought her there, took her out where she talked to the police, and then they left with the coroner. I was, by then, thinking that it was time for me to get away from here with or without Jordan. This was where I would have to wake up and smell the coffee. These women and his extracurricular activities could get me killed. I started thinking about moving as soon as possible.

It wasn't easy to just leave, especially after the attack. Jordan was as shook up as I was. He and his friends wanted me with him every night now. They'd call me, if he didn't, to tell me that they had just dropped him home and for me to go to him. Nobody wanted him to be at home alone. Since I was there every night, I moved more of my things in, and forgot about leaving, because he needed me. So did his friends.

My heavenly bubble was finally burst when Fontana called again and asked him could she and her kids come and visit again. Of course, when "walk-on-water" (as I secretly called her) came, she needed somewhere to stay, so he asked me to stay at my mom's house until she left.

"Why can't she stay at a motel?" I asked.

"She has her two little boys with her," he said.

"And?" I asked.

"That will cost more money in a motel or hotel," he said.

I was not sure whether or not that was true, but I agreed. Kids that young could usually stay for free; but hurt and upset, I packed my things and went to my mom's. Then, feeling foolish, I went to hang out with his friends. They seemed to be more upset than I was.

"Let's go out to the apartment. That's your man. You shouldn't have to wait for her to leave to talk to him," Nan said, and off to his apartment we went. He wasn't there. "He probably is out with a third woman," I remember thinking.

The next day Jordan called me and asked me to pick him up. "You want me to just blow the horn?" I asked, thinking I shouldn't have let them talk me into going to his place. If he ever wanted to commit to someone else, I must let him go.

"No, I won't hear you blowing. Come in and get me," he said.

I arrived and he answered the door. I heard Fontana doing what she was famous for, yelling at the kids and at him too.

"You need to put on a sweater or a jacket," she yelled at him, "It's suppose to be cold today and you …."

"Shut up," he said, very irritated. She zipped it up immediately.

"Well I guess she can't walk on water," I thought. "She really is a fussing, yelling chick, and she isn't getting any more respect than anyone else," I continued thinking. She must have known what I was thinking, because she asked him for a good-bye kiss as we walked out the door. He kissed her, and then we left. I was hurt again. We made our rounds to his friends' houses, and then we checked into a motel.

"OK. She doesn't walk on water," I thought again. After she went back home, I found little notes taped all over the apartment.

"She did that on purpose, you know," Jordan reminded me.

"I know," I said.

"And you left your clothes in the downstairs closet on purpose too," he said laughing.

"Not really. I thought I checked every closet," I said seriously.

"Yeah, right," he said sarcastically, but smiling.

"I wonder where the f--- Jeremy is. He was suppose to have his a— here an hour ago," Jordan said as he was trying to light up a cigarette.

"Why are you trying to smoke now? And when did you start cussing like that?" I asked, remembering how impressed I was with the fact that he didn't smoke or cuss and he was so sophisticated.

"Somebody else just said something to me about my starting to cuss. Huh. I guess things are starting to get too nerve wrecking around here. I need a cigarette or something, but I will try to stop cussing," he said.

"I bet I can guess who was mimicking me," I thought to myself.

Sweet Scorpion
100

Chapter 5:
IMAGE or VIOLENCE

Things were back to normal, again, until one morning when I was getting ready to leave for work. A girl knocked at the door. It was Paula.

"Hi," she said when he opened the door.

"What's up?" Jordan asked as he introduced us.

"I just came to tell you that I'm getting married," she said.

"Yeah, and I'm moving out west," I interrupted.

"Well, looks like you're going to be left here by yourself," I said to Jordan.

"Listen to you," he said.

"Oh, well," I said, not wanting to leave, but I couldn't be late. So I tried to be strong and left him alone with her. Later, after work, I had a flat tire, right down the street from my mom's house. A handsome gentleman in a new Jaguar pulled over to help me. He changed my tire and then followed me to my mom's. We sat on my mom's porch talking.

Suddenly I heard a horn blow. It was Jeremy and Nan. They pulled over to chat a minute, then left. My mom lived on the most driven down street in the city. So I guess I should have been inside. About a half an hour later Jordan and Darren showed up. Darren got out and went across the street, while Jordan came up onto the porch. My Jaguar friend got up and left as soon as I told him that it was my boyfriend who had just driven up.

"Who was he, a new boyfriend?" Jordan asked.

"No, I just met him," I said.

"Why did he leave, if he was 'just a friend'?" Jordan asked.

"I got with you because my boyfriend cheated on me. What makes you think I'm going to keep putting up with all your girlfriends?" I asked.

Jordan slapped me once ... twice ... and then his ring and nails hit my eye socket. I felt blood.

"Mom", I yelled, remembering Erin's mom saving her.

Jordan ran and jumped in his car when my mom came to the door. My mom butterfly bandaged my face, and put ice on my eye.

The phone rang. It was Nan. "How are you doing?" she asked.

"My whole family is upset," I said.

"He asked us what you were doing and we told him you were sitting on the porch with some dude. I didn't know he was going to clown you," she said, apologetically.

"Now what am I going to do? I love him and they're ready to lynch him," I cried.

"He's right here. He wants to talk to you," she said.

"Hi," he said.

"I'm sorry. I didn't mean to hurt you," he said. "Who was he anyway?"

"I just met him. He changed my flat tire," I said.

"Well, I'm sorry. I probably owed you one though, for some other dude," he said, laughing.

"You're silly. How am I going to clear this up, over here?" I asked.

"I don't know. My family and friends are upset too. They know you're not used to this type of thing. They're scared you're going to have me arrested," he said.

"You don't have to worry about that," I responded.

"You still love me baby?" he asked in his BS, but sincere voice.

"Yes," I said.

"I meant to spank you, because I know I owed you one. I really didn't mean to hurt you. I'm sorry for real," he said laughing.

"You ain't funny," I said, laughing. "Now I have to go calm everybody down."

"That's why you shouldn't be living there," he said.

"It's your fault, I'm back and forth," I said.

"Yeah, well," he said. "I've got to go calm my people down, too. I'll talk to you later," he said, and hung up.

In the meantime, my three brothers and my father were having a family pow-wow. They were really pissed. But when my father saw me on the phone, I heard him say, "First of all, ya'll don't even have any guns. Secondly, if you go and try to shoot up his house, you'll probably hit your sister, because she'll be in there with him. So, just leave that alone. I thought this was going to happen with the other boy and him. He needs to stay his but away from here," my dad said.

"Isn't that the boy you said had all the girlfriends and you didn't know what to do about him?" my mom asked.

"Yes," I said, knowing that I shouldn't even try that dumb excuse about his image and his friends. Maybe I should tell her he already apologized --- maybe not --- maybe tomorrow.

"Well, I think you should know what to do now. He can dish it, but he can't take it. He better not come in my house anymore," she said.

"He is such a clown," I thought. "His joking has caused too much trouble this time. He's not really the macho type." I shook my head, knowing he wasn't thinking, as usual. The doorbell rang and it was my Jaguar friend.

"Oh man," he said when he saw my

blackened eye and my butterfly bandaged face. "I'm sorry. If I had stayed, this wouldn't have happened," he said. "Is he coming back? I feel so responsible for this. Come ride with me. I feel like watching over you now," he said.

"I'll be alright. He wasn't really mad. He was living up to what his friends expected of him," I said, although that still was a BS excuse.

"Come ride with me," he said. I went, thinking, "Maybe, I should get out of this now."

My Jaguar friend took me to meet his sister with whom he shared a house. He told her everything that happened. They were both so apologetic. I eventually met his entire family. They were all nice, with nice places, and nice expensive cars. I was impressed, but I think he was an old player and I believe he had other women somewhere. Old players are not honest like Jordan. I went to work with my injured eye and had to listen to my co-workers tell me about all their knock-down, drag-out fights that they'd had with their husbands. They acted as if fighting, not just arguing, was a normal thing. They told me that they always fought back, which I didn't do. My sister had told me that if you hit men back, they hit you again. She had told me to never fight back because it made them madder, and she said men hit harder than women. But these girls took pride in getting in good hits and throwing stuff, and of course they loved making up. This was not something I was going to get use to, either way. They tried to make me feel comfortable at work though, but I used my face as an excuse to take a vacation, after first telling them I needed time off due to a nervous breakdown.

Jordan's friends laughed saying, "You really are having a nervous breakdown. You just don't know it."

I didn't feel nervous or crazy, but I knew that I should be getting myself away from him. I shouldn't have been putting up with him doing whatever he wanted to do, so maybe I was nuts.

"I'm glad these girls are starting to eliminate themselves," Jordan finally said one day when we talked.

That gave me a spark of hope for a second. Then I wondered how many of his foolish hopefuls, were thinking he would marry them if everybody else quit. I had to get back to reality though. If he didn't move out of town with me, it might be for the best. He might bring his problems and hopeful girlfriends with him.

The first night of our reunion after "the fight," I met Jordan back at his apartment, and there was a sink and kitchen full of dirty dishes. Somebody had cooked a feast. There was an empty casserole dish with remnants of macaroni & cheese stuck to it, along with many other pots, pans, and dishes.

"Wash the dishes and clean up the kitchen for me," Jordan asked.

"Oh no, I'm not," I said, thinking you better bring whoever made this mess back here to clean it up. "I'm not cleaning up after your girlfriends," I said.

"Yeah, okay," he said as we went up to bed. "Don't touch me. You'll climb all over me, but you won't wash the dishes. Don't touch me," he said as he turned his back to me.

"I don't even care," I thought. "He'll have whoever it was over again when I'm not around anyway. She might as well come back and clean up after herself. I will just do without you tonight partner, 'because I'll feel like a fool doing that," I kept thinking, and I turned over and went to sleep.

Now that I was off from work, I was available to try to sit up under him all day. I was with him when he stopped by all the ladies' places, and was there when they all stopped by his place. I came back from my mom's house one evening and a girl named Brenda was there with him. He had mentioned her a few days before, saying that her man had just left for college the day before, and she was already trying to give him some. He never turned down any woman though, even if he thought she was wrong.

For some reason, I felt like I could be demanding respect, so I said, "What are you doing with a girl here?" not directing any meanness towards her. I went up the stairs as I heard him say, "Uh, she doesn't usually act like that. She even let me bring my pregnant girlfriend to her apartment. Uh – I'll be right back." He chased me up the stairs as I laughed to myself. We got to the 1st floor, and he said, "What's up with you today, baby? You don't usually do this."

"I'm tired of these girls'" I whined like a baby, serious, but laughing inside. I've never made any demands before. That tantrum felt good. Maybe I should have been doing that all the time. He thought I would let him do anything, since I let him bring Tiffany to my apartment. Actually I don't regret being nice to his child's mother. I even bought her a case of diapers. She was nice. But, since he's not getting mad about this one, let me see how far I can take this. I stomped my foot a little and said "You're not ever going to get rid of all these women," and I went up to the 3rd floor with him following me.

When he caught up to me, he hugged me. "Baby, you know you're my wife. I told you she shouldn't even be trying to get with me this quick after he left. She doesn't mean anything to me," he actually pleaded.

"You love me?" I asked.

"You know I do," he said.

I didn't really believe him, but he kissed me and eventually he sent her home. So I felt like I had a little power. That was a first though. I smiled inside.

Billy came over in the morning and I answered the door. "How are you doing?" he said, really sounding concerned.

"I'm okay," I said, knowing he was thinking about my still lingering black eye.

"He told me, he is going to marry you, you know. Don't worry, things will be okay," he said.

For some reason I didn't believe him either, and he was always my biggest fan, the head of my cheerleading team. Didn't he know Jordan will say one thing today and then tomorrow let some woman change his mind? I'll be his 'unofficial' wife, forever.

The phone rang at my mom's house. "What are you doing?" Jordan asked.

"Washing my clothes."

"Tiffany had the baby."

"What was it?"

"It was a boy."

"What's his name?"

"Jermaine," he said, which was Jordan's middle name.

"Oh," I said, wondering what was going to happen next.

"I'll be there in a minute," he said.

"OK," I said happily.

"So she had a boy. Why didn't she give him your first name?" I asked.

"Uh," he hesitated.

"She did. I just didn't want to hurt you. See, I told you to have my baby a long time ago. You said 'no'," he said, and then he hugged and kissed me. "As much as we've been together, you should have been pregnant," he continued, as we stood on the basement steps, staring into the future.

Sweet Scorpion
110

Chapter 6:
THE LAST STRAW?

For a couple of weeks our friends were over everyday, talking about Darren's birthday at his new place. Darren's girlfriend was there one morning, talking about it, but said she wasn't going to attend.

"What?" I asked. "Why aren't you going?"

"I don't care what he does anymore. We're almost done," she said.

"I want to be with my man," I thought. "I'm not like her anyway. I don't think she ever cared. Plus, Jordan always had her or Jeremy and his gal babysitting me, while he ran around with other girls.

"Why doesn't he baby-sit you himself?" Jeremy asked one day when I was in the way of him trying to flirt with Nan.

"I'm not hanging out with her. I want to go with Jordan to the party," I thought as I let Darren's girlfriend out.

"I should tell on her," Jordan said.

"That's none of your business. She's not your woman," I said.

"Yeah, but that's my friend's woman," Jordan said.

"Yeah, but Jeremy's your friend too," I said.

"Darren's a really nice person. He already caught her once. She wouldn't come to the door and he looked through the window and caught her red-handed," Jordan said. "She's more street than he is. She'll dog him out."

She said that she doesn't care anymore, and they are just about over. You stay out of it. That's their business," I restated. "Besides, it looks like all these girls are doing the same thing, trying to get the same reaction that Erin got - a marriage proposal," I thought to myself. Unfortunately, some were just getting slapped around, including me.

"Am I going to the party with you?" I asked Jordan, afraid he was expecting me to not mind staying at home.

"Uh, I told Tiffany that I was taking her to the party," he said.

Very hurt, all I could think about was that he was feeling sorry for her and was considering doing the right thing by her, especially since she played her Ace card and named her baby Jordan Junior.

"You haven't seen her more than once a month, the whole nine months, if that often. Now you're taking HER to the party, not me," I said, hoping that I wasn't getting too brave.

"She – I – uh," he stumbled.

"Take both of us," I said. "You're supposed to be a player. Well, take both us," I said, hoping he would just get flattered or egomaniacal, and not mad.

He got egomaniacal and said, "Ok. Be ready by 8:00 o'clock."

"Ok. I'll be at my mother's," I said.

Eight o'clock came and Jordan rang the bell.

"You ready?" he asked.

"Yes," I said, still hurt and nervous. We got to the car and Tiffany was already sitting in the front seat. I got into the back, trying to pretend that I was strong enough not to care. She was sad and sweet as always. She looked like she would burst into tears at any minute, just like she always looked.

"Why did you stick yourself into that little girl?" I remembered Billy asking Jordan. She looked, sad, hurt, and unhappy to everybody. If she only knew, she wasn't the only person who felt that way, I was just good at hiding my feelings most of the time. I was sure some of the others were too. I was already feeling real foolish for demanding this, and we hadn't even reached the party yet. When we got into the party, Marisa, one of his other friends, was already there. Jordan, Tiffany, and I, sat on the couch right across from her. I wished I were invisible. I felt foolish.

"How's the baby?" I asked Tiffany, just making conversation while trying to camouflage my pain.

"He's fine," she said, not being successful at hiding her feelings.

Soon after, she told Jordan that she was tired and asked him if she could lie down in the bedroom. She then excused herself from the party. I got up and took the tour of the new place. There was back-to-back beautiful living room sets in a large double front room. The middle room had a pool table and a large bar that was beautifully upholstered by his parents. The double folding doors opened up to a large wooden, lighted, fish tank, with beautiful fish in it. Everything was beautiful. No one went into the bedroom though, because Tiffany was lying down in there. I played pool and danced to the music. I knew Tiffany was probably awake, feeling just as foolish as I was feeling. She was probably thinking that her Ace card had gotten trumped, but I was thinking that I shouldn't have come. Both of us didn't have to be hurting, although Marisa was there, too. Marisa had told Jordan she wouldn't have any parts of a non-monogamous boyfriend, and she had already been in trouble with her boyfriend about Jordan; but it still mattered to me that she was there without her man. So I still might have been feeling foolish even if he hadn't brought Tiffany, and she would have felt the same without me.

We got into the car after the party and Jordan's friend, Duck, asked to be dropped home.

He got in the back with me, and then Jordan drove off. When it looked like we were going in my mom's direction, I said, "Don't take me home first."

"Yes I am taking you home first," he said, "it's on the way." I knew then that he was probably taking her back to his apartment instead of me.

"See you guys later," I said, knowing that "when" had finally arrived. If I didn't come first in his life, I was no longer going to stay around. I got on the plane for Hollywood, the next day. I called my job and verbally turned in my resignation and painfully tried to plan my new life. I wanted to go back to school, so I started looking into the application process at the nearby state university. Of course, every minute of everyday, I thought of Jordan. I finally called Billy and told him where I was, giving him my number to give to Jordan. There was never a phone at the apartment since the Puerto Rican girl blocked all his calls, so I called Nan a few days later and she said, "He's walking around here saying 'she'll be back. She can't stay away from me.'"

"Yeah, right," I thought. "I'm not coming back, for real," I said.

"Ring," the phone rang the next day.

"Hello," I said.

"Why did you leave like that?" he said.

"You took Tiffany home with you after Darren's party, didn't you?" I asked, still crazy in love.

"Did I?" he said, probably not really

knowing why I left.

"Baby, you've got to come home now. I need you," he pleaded.

"I already quit my job Jordan. I'm tired. I'm going back to school, out here. Why don't you move up here with me? Your brother is only a few hours from me. You could be up here close to him," I pleaded back.

"I'm not ready to make that move yet," he said.

"I don't want to come back there. It's nice here," I said.

"You'll be back. I know you will. You can't stay away from me," he said.

I wanted to cry, because I knew I couldn't continue to be foolish, plus I didn't have a roundtrip ticket, anyway. If he had told me he was going to the airport to pay my way back, I might have foolishly went back to him. Thank goodness he didn't think of that. I began my new job and opened up several credit card accounts. I started looking for an apartment. I still hoped I could convince Jordan to move to California to be with me. I bought him things and mailed them to him, including a gold ring with his initials in small diamonds. I had one also, with my initials. "These are our wedding rings," I wrote.

I sent him hundreds of pictures of me, including one of me in a set of footy PJs with big white rollers in my hair. I knew better than to take a picture in those ugly pink ones, but I wanted him to remember me as the domestic one he came home to (after I sent him the ones with me in pretty clothes, of course.) Finally, during pre-Christmas week, I called his mom's house. His brother answered the phone. He had flown home for Christmas. He gave me Jordan's number. I called.

"Hi. Don't you miss me?" I whined.

"Yes. I miss you. Are you here?" he asked.

"No," I said.

"You're not coming home for Christmas?" he whined back.

"No. I wasn't," I said.

"Billy and Erin are having a New Year's Eve party. You missed my Scorpio party. Don't you want to bring the New Year in with me?" he asked.

"You want me to come?" I asked.

"Yes," he said sweetly.

"Ok. Let me see what I can do," I said.

"You re-a-lly miss me?" I asked whiningly.

"Ye-es. Really," he said.

I knew he had to miss me. I was always there for him, unquestionably, anytime he needed me, comforting him whenever he needed to feel "home safe."

"I'll call you back tomorrow with the details," I said.

The next day, I called him with my travel details. "Pick me up at 6:30 A.M., TWA arrivals," I said.

I waited about a half hour before I called to see if Jordan had forgotten that he was supposed to be picking me up. "I'm at the airport. Did you forget?"

"Ok, baby. I'll be there," he said. When he arrived he smiled, as he was getting my luggage.

"The west coast has been good to you, baby," he said as he kissed me.

"I guess", I said knowing I'd been pampering myself a bit, for a change.

We arrived at a different apartment and he got my things out of the trunk. "I was paranoid of the other place without you here," he said, as I looked puzzled.

When he unlocked the door, he told me to have a seat in the living room and went to the bedroom. I heard whispering and someone moving around on the bed.

"No, he didn't," I'm thinking. Ten minutes later, he brought out a thin brown-skinned little girl who looked like she still jumped double-dutch in the school yard. He started to ask me to take her home, but I gave him that look and he just called her a cab.

"How old was she?" I asked.

"She's old enough. She's 19," he said.

"Why didn't you take her home BEFORE you picked me up?" I asked.

"I didn't want to make you wait," he said seriously, like he really thought he made the right decision, picking me up first.

"I thought you said the girls were eliminating themselves," I said, wondering how many new ones he had met.

In the bathroom, there was a potty chair and some other baby things were scattered around the apartment.

"Why did Tiffany leave?" I asked.

"I only told her to stay here when I went out of town like you use to do, but when I came back, she had moved in, saying that her family had put her out. I just asked her to find someplace else for her and the kids to stay. I couldn't take it any longer," he said, not really convincing me on the 'she moved in while I was gone, part'. This was the family property. His brother's baby's mama lived in the apartment next door. I think he was trying to do the right thing by taking care of his own, until he had to live there with her himself. I must admit though, he probably would have let her stay, if I had been with him, providing him someplace else to live, when business started going bad. She was set free though. That was better for her, although she probably didn't think so at the time.

I looked in the yellow pages to try to find me a beautician and he went to sleep. I went to get my hair done and was back before he woke up. An hour later, Fanny, another girlfriend of Jordan's, knocked on the door.

"Good, I want to use your car" he said, as he let her in.

"Oh, that Fanny," I said.

"Erin," she said. "I didn't know you were the Erin he's always talking about.

"Where do you two know each other from?" he asked.

"High school and we were neighbors," I said.

"Good. Keep each other company," he said. "I've got somewhere to go," he said. "I'm taking your car Fanny," he said as he took her keys. Then the phone rang. Fanny answered it. "Hello."

"It's for you Jordan," she said.

"Who is it?" he asked.

"May I ask who's calling?" Fanny asked.

"Huh. She said no," Fanny said.

"What?" I said in unison with Jordan.

"Hello," Jordan said.

"Ah. Hi. That was Fanny and Erin. What's up? Ok, that will be helpful. Talk to you later. Bye," he said as he hung up.

"Who was that?" Fanny and I said.

"That was just Fontana. She's cra-, never mind. I'll be back," he said and left.

Fanny and I took the time to reminisce about high school days. Then out of no where, she started crying. "I would come over here when Tiffany and her kids were here, and he was just aggravated all the time. I would do her hair for her, trying to help her look pretty for him, but I think having kids around was nothing he was ready for. His son was just a baby, but her husbands' son was running around screaming and tearing up stuff. You know, just being a normal kid. Jordan wasn't use to that. I tried to take up for her, but he just sent her home," Fanny said, wiping her eyes.

"So then I thought sure I had a clear chance with him, since I don't have any children, but then he told me that he was going to buy that broad on the phone, Fontana, or whatever her name is, an engagement ring for her birthday in March. She has two kids that ain't none of his," and she started crying again.

I couldn't help it but she made me cry too. I was not just feeling sorry for her, but I was also hurt from what she had just told me. He's going to marry "walk-on-water" anyway, the one who allegedly "lost" his twins. She was the only mean evil one in the bunch, and he chose her. We tried to dry our tears and then began wondering where he was. It was 4:00 A.M. and he wasn't home yet. I knew he was spending the night with one of the many phone calls that came. New replacements had taken the places of all those who had eliminated themselves. Fanny was a very pretty girl. She had pinkish ivory skin, but she had a little weight problem. She was real sweet and I could tell she really loved him. I tried to tell myself that I had a better chance than she. I didn't have any children either. He might not care about her weight, because she was so pretty, but she knew her way around the streets. She was real sweet and nice, but he liked them square. He trusted squares better. But, she was too nice to distrust though. "Yoo-Who," I thought. "Wake Up. He's not marrying either one of us. He's buying that evil, loud, cussing one, an engagement ring, and marrying <u>her</u>."

He finally came home about 8:00 A.M. Fanny took her car keys and left. I didn't mention what Fanny had told me, but he told me that Fontana had called. She was coming into town for the New Year's Eve party too.

"She needs a place for her and the kids to stay," he said. Feeling déjà vu, I said, again, "Why can't she stay at a motel?"

"There's no money for that. She's got two kids," he said "and you do have somewhere else you can go. You can go to your family's house," he said.

"They don't even know I'm here," I said.

"Erin," he said. "Please."

"Ok," I said, knowing, he was never going to change. I was never coming back here, after this nightmare reunion. That night Operetta, my old friend, and I went to midnight mass. It was a real nice service. I saw one of Jordan's friends there with his girlfriend. I thought how nice that was and wondered if Jordan would have gone with me if I had asked him. I went to my mom's sometime that week. They were surprised to see me. My friends called me about a couple of funerals and a party. Billy and Erin pulled up to my mom's house when I was on my way out to a party. They wanted to know where the party was. I told them I didn't know.

"I'm going to go pick up Operetta. She knows where it is, I don't," I said, not wanting Jordan to show up and spoil my evening.

"Jordan said for you to call him," Billy said.

"Ok", I said, wondering, "what does he want with me? Why doesn't he just stay with "walk-on-water" and leave me alone?"

We went to a party where one of our pro-basketball player friends lived. He was glad to see me, but I had dated his body guard (who was no longer around), so he wasn't a person of interest, but Jordan didn't need to be there with me.

The next day, Billy, Jordan, and Erin came to pick me up. I guess Fontana was at his house with the kids. We went out to the club. All the old fellas were there. They all got up and hugged me. The guy I saw at church was there.

"Hi. I saw you at midnight mass the other day," I said.

He looked embarrassed because I said that in front of his 'boys' and said, "Yeah, my girl wanted me to go with her."

I didn't know that would embarrass him. I'm a girl, what did I know. Anyway, they all made me feel good and I enjoyed myself, but I knew that I was never coming back, regardless of how much his "friends" loved me. Jordan didn't know what I was thinking and I didn't bother telling him, so we went to a motel and Fontana was left at the apartment with her kids all night, as usual.

We woke in the morning and went our separate ways. "I'll see you at the party tonight," he said.

I picked up Erin's sister from the city and went way to the outskirts to Billy and Erin's place.

None of my friends would go with me. They knew what Jordan had done, and told me that I needed to tell him to take a hike. I also found myself at another party with him and another woman.

When midnight came, while everyone was on the balcony yelling and celebrating, I slipped out the door and went home. "I guess he didn't learn anything from the last party," I thought. I guess I didn't either, because I should have left him the day before both parties, not the day after. He was totally not paying any attention to what he was doing.

All the next day, I was in and out. My family told me that Jordan had called five or six times. I couldn't call him back because Tiffany's family made her cut the phone off, since she didn't live there anymore. He caught up with me, as I and my closest friends were going out to one last party, before my boarding the plane back home. "When did you leave the party?" he asked.

"You looked pretty occupied to me. When did you notice that I was gone?" I asked, not really wanting to care anymore.

"Ah, baby. What cha doing now?" he asked.

"My friends are over here. We're going club hopping," I said.

"Pick me up tomorrow around 10:00 A.M.," he said.

"Ok", I said, hesitatingly considering it and wondering if Fontana was going to be there yelling again. I was trying to figure out what he liked about her that I didn't have. Maybe I should have straight out asked him to marry me like she did a thousand times, instead of waiting on him to ask me. She did have the gift of gab in her letters. Maybe she finally convinced him she was the one for him. She said that she thought she was the one strong enough for him, since she had been through so much, so young. Maybe I needed to act tougher. Maybe being strong enough to be "unfriendly" with the rest of the girls, made him think she wasn't dumb enough to let him think his BS was ok. But I also read about all the pretty girls he had around her when he visited her out of town, and she complained about him not spending time with her; and, he even, just yesterday, asked me to move to the town where she lives. I'm not leaving the warm west coast weather. He could be moving her west with his brother for all I know, and just wants someone in that town when he visits. I don't know what she had that I didn't, but I didn't pick him up in the morning. I got on the airplane and I wasn't going to look back.

"Billy," I said, "Tell Jordan that I'm at home."

"At your moms?" he asked.

"No. Out west," I said.

"Ok, baby. You're out there where it's warm," he said.

"Yeah. I can do without that cold weather," I said.

Later that day, Jordan called. "Why did you leave?" he asked angrily.

"You told Fanny that you were marrying Fontana. Why would I stay there with you?" I said.

"I didn't tell her that," he yelled.

"She said you told her that you were planning on buying Fontana an engagement ring for her birthday in March," I said.

"You know I'm not marrying Fontana. I just told Fanny that because she was getting too comfortable. You know that wasn't true," he said.

"I shouldn't have told her that and she shouldn't have told you that," he said, still very angry.

"My friends are teasing me, saying that I can't keep up with my woman," he said, pleading.

"All you're worried about is what your friends think of you – your image," I said. "You're marrying Fontana, leave me alone," I said.

"I'm not marrying her, I told you. Listen girl – huh – wait. My brother wants to talk to you," he said.

"Hi baby," Rick said.

"I'm sending him out there okay. He's going nuts. I'll call you back with the time to pick him up okay," he said softly.

"OK Rick," I said. He called back an hour later with a time and an airline details.

"Lord," I prayed. "I've got to be strong enough to say this is over. He's never going to change. He'll get me home and do the same things. He's so mad; he might beat me up at the airport, anyway. If you don't think he'll get rid of all those girls and marry me – give me a sign and I won't go to the airport," I continued to pray. The friend I chose to take me to the airport had car trouble and didn't make it. My car was still at home where my parents and Jordan were. I had made arrangements, while I was there, for it to be driven to me, but it hadn't arrived yet. I could have gotten another ride, but I took that as a sign from God. Jordan was always going to be a thoughtless, selfish playboy.

The phone rang at the time of the plane's arrival. I refused to answer it. It rang for a couple of hours. I couldn't care, even though I did. I knew my decision had probably pissed him, his family, and his friends off, especially since they spent money to send him to me; but I just couldn't care. I went with God. I sent Jordan's Brother Rick a telegram, telling him that, "I am sorry, but he had to let me go because his brat brother wasn't going to wake up and give me the love, respect, and commitment that he demanded for himself. He didn't want to share me with anyone, and I didn't want to share him with anyone either. I wanted him to marry me, for real, just like all the rest of the girls did. He may or may not be marrying Fontana. Either way, he was not ready to settle down with me. That's ok, because if you're not ready for marriage, but get married anyway, there is more pain to be endured. So with that being the case, Jordan has to let me go," I continued to plead with Rick in so many words.

I can't blame Fontana for straight out asking him to marry her. She was probably just a mean person because of what she had been through with her children's father. He took care of her, but he didn't marry her after the 1st baby, then she had a

2nd and still no proposal. She was upset about that, and then she was going through the same thing again, with four times the women. After "losing" the twins, her only Ace card was her gift of gab and/or Rick's wife. My only Ace was my intelligence, and I was losing that, being dumb, putting up with all those girls. I had to use my Ace for my own life. I couldn't be mad about Tiffany either. I would have used her Ace if I had been in her shoes, but I was infertile. I couldn't get pregnant and under those circumstances, I'm glad I couldn't. Jordan and I had no children when we met. Maybe I was living in a dream world, but I hoped, like most women, to have mine with the person I would be married to forever. And Jordan had started making babies without me, with other people.

Chapter 7:
MOVED ON

It took a couple of years, but I finally stopped thinking of Jordan every time I needed a hug. I finally went back to college and after graduating from junior college, I joined the Air Force in order to continue school. I was a semester from my Bachelors' degree, when I asked for orders to Korea. I was dating a wavy haired playboy lieutenant who I tried to hold at bay platonically, because I refused to have my heart and mind clouded with a lack of commitment. I wanted to get away from him too, so I got a transfer. The only problem with that move was that graduation got postponed.

When I got to Korea, I did get married to a guy from home that I only knew one month. He had custody of two sons that called me Mama. They were seven and eight, and plenty of fun. Since it was my

2nd legal marriage I tried to be a little more tolerant than during my teenage marriage, but their dad and I couldn't make it work. It seemed he really was looking for a nanny, not a wife to spend time with and have more babies. He changed his mind about us having a daughter as soon as the doctors gave me the fertility pills.

When I married my 3rd husband, the doctors were already trying to figure out why I couldn't get pregnant. They put me through several tests with Petri dishes, microscopes, and fertility pills. During my third marriage, I finally had three children, two boys and one girl. My husband already had three other daughters with two other women and he acted as if my children didn't mean much to him. I was very unhappy, but our little family looked perfect to everybody else; and I wanted stability for our children, therefore I stayed. He continued to sleep in his room alone, but he was an intelligent nerd, could play the guitar and the piano, and could build/repair anything. He wasn't a drunk, drug addict, chronic womanizer, or violent woman beater. Therefore, I thought it was a fair trade off for sleeping alone.

I finally couldn't stand it any longer. I was determined to find out why my husband was so unaffectionate. His mother was always hugging and kissing my kids. He had to grow up with affection. I kept hearing rumors that I belonged to some man who wanted me for himself and didn't want anyone sleeping with me. That wasn't true, nor was it my husband's problem. He was the same way with his other wives. He hardly ever slept with them either. But, I did hear similar rumors when I divorced my 2nd husband. Maybe there was someone somewhere stirring up trouble and trying to get me back. I began thinking that I wouldn't have a permanent, normal relationship until I followed up on those rumors. But I couldn't find Jordan after that divorce, so I tried to go on with my life. Frustrated again with hearing the rumors during my 3rd marriage, I had my brother find Jordan for me, but I changed my mind about contacting him. I was scared he would be more of a jinx, than a blessing.

Two months later my husband got hit by an 18 wheeler tractor trailer truck, while he was at work on the side of a road. He had nine broken bones and three surgeries. I thought he would become more humble and stop being so mean, but he got worse. His ex-wife and his little fling from the year before started calling our house daily to check up on him. I allowed the 2 women to call only because he was injured. Eventually, he went from bedridden, to wheelchair, to walker, to crutches, then to cane. But he began being sneaky with the calls, especially from his ex-wife. He was giving me the impression that he may have wanted to divorce me and reconcile with her. He also would roll his wheelchair up to his car, crawl in, throw his chair in the car; then go to meet his fling and her friends. It seemed that since he had a near death experience, he wanted his freedom. I decided this might be the time to get brave enough to call my old friend, because, like with Angelo, I needed someone to ease my pain.

Jordan's mother was blind. She had seen his older sister, but had not seen Jordan or his brother. She lost her eyesight after having her first child. When I called her house, she took a while feeling her way to the phone. I almost chickened out and was about to hang up when her familiar voice answered the phone.

"He's not here. Can I take a message?" she asked.

"Tell him Erin called" I said. "Can I leave a message for him to call me?"

A few days passed and then on New Year's Eve day, Jordan called. We talked and laughed for over an hour. I felt like 100 lbs had been lifted off my shoulders. I felt free from the shell I had crawled into, when I got away from him. It had been 16 years since I heard that voice. He sounded just the same. I felt the same way I did 16 years ago even though he was 3000 miles away. There was a smile on my face that hadn't been there in years.

That smiled pissed my husband off, though. It was okay for his two women to call him, and it was okay for him to ask me to leave the room while his nurse bathed him (instead of letting me bathe him), but it was not okay for me to be smiling after talking to my long lost friend, long distance.

That night, my husband, my kids, my brother's family and myself, spent the night at a friend's for the New Year's Eve celebration, somewhere in Oakland or San Jose. We played games, danced, and had fun. I felt liberated and extremely happy. My husband was frowning, being his evil self all during the party. He seemed to get more irritated if he saw me beaming and enjoying myself. During the next three months, my husband and I discussed our separation. He just announced one day that he was going to move into the weekly motel where the manager hired him to work occasionally, and where he met his fling.

"OK", I said. I started my plan to move back to Southern California to promote my music and my first book. I submitted resumes and sent for applications. I had my income tax done and was all set for the move. When I finally got there and got settled in my apartment, I called Jordan again. "So you chose to be happy and single, rather than married and miserable," he said.

"I have three children Jordan. I have to make decisions that won't mess up their lives. I thought being with a stable family with both their parents was better for them. I wasn't supposed to be selfish and think only of me and just what I needed," I said.

"Yeah well, sometimes peace of mind is better than anything else. The kids would rather see you happy, than miserable," he said.

"So when are you coming to visit me? I told you to bring your gal and you guys could have stayed with me and my husband for a weekend," I said.

"Yeah, and I would have been trying to push you into a room to get some, when he wasn't looking," he laughed. "Besides I don't want to come for a weekend. What schools do they have up there?" he asked.

"What would be your major?" I asked.

"Paralegal, but I don't want a school that's not accredited. I may want to transfer into a 4-year college later and I want all my credits to go with me. I don't want to waste any time," he said.

"Why are you just now going back to school?" I thought you'd have your accounting degree, by now," I said.

"I don't want to do accounting anymore. I'm pretty versed on legal matters. My lawyer wanted me to move to Maryland with him and get into the paralegal program, but I declined," he said.

"Why did you decline? I was surprised to hear that you were still in that town. What about all those people that were shooting at you?" I asked.

"They are all gone. I'm cool now. I don't even need to carry my protection or have my men around anymore," he said.

"Where are Jeremy and Billy?" I asked.

"They both moved out of town. Billy came back for a while, but he moved back out of here," he said.

"What about Erin?" I asked.

"You know that wasn't gonna last. She had fallen in love with my brother, after waiting for Billy so long. She moved out of town too, but not with either one of them," he said. "She's in Kansas somewhere."

"I heard that you were in Kansas with a big accounting executive job," I said, remembering when I divorced my second husband, I was nervous about reuniting with him, thinking about how sophisticated and conservative he was when I first met him.

"No I haven't been to Kansas, but I have been to California, looking for you a couple of times," he said.

"What parts of California were you looking in, and when? I've lived from the LA valley to way north of Sacramento, and my kids were born in central California," I said.

"You should have come here when I first left there. I knew you were paranoid that my sister would have that woman's crazy husband up here, but I've never seen any of them up here. My sister didn't know him anyway, her old man did. I did see Fontana's in-laws up here though, but my dad knew them before Fontana did, and they were his friends when he was a kid. If I warned you about that other guy shooting up the courtroom, what makes you think I would let anything happen to you? I wanted to get you away from the women, and from danger. What happened to that guy, anyway?" I asked.

"That crazy fool went to prison and got himself killed. I don't know where his wife ended up," he said.

"And how do you know I was paranoid? I did come up there, after you left so abruptly," he said.
"Yeah. Well, I was paranoid by then. I learned paranoia from you anyway. You were a little too

mad. You might have beaten me up at the airport," I laughed.

"Where is Fontana, by the way?" I asked.

"She's married to some guy and she's got a little girl now. She called me a few years ago to cuss me out for dating her ex's cousin. I told her 'married self', that what I do was none of her business, but she said she didn't want me no where near her and her family," he said. "She's crazy."

"No she's not. She didn't want you messing up her mind again, or her relationship," I said, thinking she's still a fussy butt, but she's right. "Where are your kids and their mothers?" I asked.

"My daughter's mother has 6 kids now and they never told her about me, just to keep her husband from getting upset. So, I haven't seen her. My son's mother broke up with her husband when I started going around visiting my son. But, I already had a girlfriend, so it got a little dramatic around here for a minute", he said.

"See. You got back into her head again and she broke up her marriage, because of you this time," I said.

"Yeah well. I guess I wasn't thinking," he said as if he just now had thought about it.

"Yeah. Again not thinking," I said.

"Hey, where's that girl you had in the bed that day when I came home for Christmas?" I remembered.

"She owns a couple of businesses around town. I took one of my girlfriends to patronize her, and she politely whispered to me to never hurt her by bringing another woman into her establishment again. I was just trying to bring her some business, although she's doing quite well for herself. Her husband helped set her up in business. I didn't think she'd care," he said.

"Good for her, but I guess she remembers the joy and the pain of being with and without you," I said.

"Anyway, how soon do you want to start school?"

"Just let me know what they have available and I'll let you know when I'm coming," he said.

"Love you," he said.

"Love you, too," I said.

I received disability from being in the Air Force, but I would not receive child support until the kid's dad started getting his annuity payments and/or got a job, which was not until the end of the year, months away. I went to my unemployment hearing and they turned me down in the appeal procedure. I wasn't going to walk out of there without expressing my disagreement with their decision, because I didn't get food stamps for the kids because I was suppose to get unemployment. I had no way to feed my children. My job was a government contract job and I left when they told us the contract was ending. I got upset and argued with the adjudicator, but to no avail. When the kids and I got back to the apartment, I called Jordan. He had experienced a similar incident that day at the same time. We laughed, although upset.

"Maybe we belong together," he said.

"The two schools that I registered you in keep calling everyday, wondering when you will be starting," I said knowing that with no money, I would probably be on my way back home soon, anyway. I couldn't pay bills and feed three kids with that little disability check. I would have to give up and retreat to my parent's home, 3000 miles away.

Coincidently I arrived home on my 1st boyfriend Bob's birthday, but I didn't call him. I had just recently heard that he had moved back home and I wasn't sure whether or not he was still with his second wife. I didn't call Jordan the first day either. I think I was a little nervous. I hadn't actually seen him in 17 years, though we had been talking on the phone almost a year. The next afternoon I got brave enough to call him and we made a date for me to pick him up. When he opened the door and came down the steps, he was dressed in a nice leisure suit. He looked very distinguished, different, but handsome. He certainly still had his sweet talking voice and self assured manner. My children were with me and since it was a warm autumn day, we went to the park. We talked and played at the park everyday almost. When the kids went to sleep at night, we would go back out and play cards with his friends. We had a problem though; he still lived with his girlfriend.

"I'm not letting you touch me until you move out," I said. "I'm not a home wrecker or a mistress," I said.

"You need to give me some incentive to move out," he began sweet talking me and grabbing for my chest.

"By the way, what happened to your torpedoes? You had big breasts. Have you been on crack or something?"

"I've never done any crack. Do I look like or act like a crack head?" I said.

"You are kinda thin. Besides there are some professional people way out there on that stuff now, both males and females," he said.

"You're right," I said, knowing of some surprising folks on that stuff, myself.

"I'm just allergic to everything - sugar, cheese, milk, meat, you name it. So I lost a lot of weight and I can't gain an ounce."

"I've got to go in early tonight," Jordan said.

"She's starting to think that it's Eunice, I'm sneaking around with. She's asking questions."

"Yeah well, I don't do this. It's making me uncomfortable. We are something special, but I still want you to hurry and move out. I don't do this," I said.

"You live with your mama and neither one of us have a job. Where am I going to live?" he said.

"Go live with your mama," I said.

"She lives in a one bedroom apartment and she's not supposed to have a roomer," he said.

"What a pair," I said. "My job starts after the new year. Maybe we can start looking for a place now."

He kissed me. "See you tomorrow," he said and walked around the corner.

"Who's going to finance this romance?" I looked up to the heavens to ask God.

The next morning, Jordan called. "Let's go to this temp service. You can work for them until your job starts. This place usually puts me to work immediately," he said.

We both got jobs that day. I worked for a USA Today on the night shift, because my mom didn't mind me leaving the kids as long as they were asleep. He worked the day shift at a factory. At least two evenings a week when I picked Jordan up from work he would say, "Hi kids. How about pizza tonight?" and we would go to the pizza place for dinner.

"We like pineapple on our pizza," the kids said the first day.

"Pineapple? Ok, I'll try it on my pan pizza," Jordan said.

"Hey. I like this," Jordan smiled, and then ordered it every time after that. The next time he said, "How about pizza kids," I was very short on money.

"Be quiet," I said. "You never pay for it. How do you know I have money?" "What do you do with your money anyway?" I asked. "You get paid every week."

"How do you know that I'm not saving my money for a special surprise for you?" he said.

"Actually when we put the kids to bed tonight, I need to have a serious talk with you. 9:30, okay?" he said.

"Okay," I said wondering what he had up. I was actually thinking he was going to demand that I not wait until he moved out to have sex with him – and I was thinking about changing my mind anyway.

When I picked him up we went to his half sister's apartment first. They just found out about her recently, so to spend time with her, we would play cards at her place sometimes.

"Let's go," Jordan said.

"I thought you guys were playing cards tonight," Jenny said.

"We have a date tonight," Jordan said.

"Umh. Have fun," she smiled.

Jordan always drove, especially at night, although he didn't have a driver's license. He stopped at different friends' houses, ran in for a minute, and then he finally stopped at a spot where he went everyday. He never took me in.

"I know you're wondering why I stop over here in this neighborhood everyday," he said.

"Yes," but I had an idea already.

"I am on drugs. I have a serious habit, that's why I never have any money. I thought it was time for me to be honest with you," he said.

"So why haven't you tried a rehab?"

"I am going to try rehab soon. I just haven't got around to it yet," he said.

"So when did you start doing drugs?" I asked.

"I was falling on hard times and this chick I was with, turned me on to it," he said.

"You never dated girls that used drugs. I was told once, that you were dating some girl with a wild name like "cool mama" or "big bad mama", or something. I knew then, you must have been losing your mind," I laughed.

"Ha! That's what my family said. Where did you get 'that' girl from?" they kept saying."

"So how long has this been going on?" I asked.

"Only about five years. I know I can kick it. I'm really getting tired of my life being screwed up, but I need your help," he said.

"Ok," I said, thinking of the VA's program. "Is this our planned date?" I asked.

"'Fraid it is," he continued. "Sorry baby. That's why I couldn't move to California and start school. I was going to go to rehab first, but I kept putting it off, and then you came home."

I got the details of the rehab at the VA and for months tried to convince Jordan to go check himself into the program. In the meantime his girlfriend found out who I was and things got worse. She knew I didn't approve of drugs, so she started having drug parties at her house every weekend to keep him hooked and away from me.

"Mom, do you think I'm wasting my time trying to rehab him," I asked Jordan's mother, as I drove her to the clinic. "She keeps his druggie friends at their house to keep him from going to rehab," I told her.

"She knows he's talking about going to rehab because of me. I may be making it worse for him. She's giving him more, because of me too. She even told her kids not to wake him up when I call him to get up and get ready for work," I said.

"Yeah. She won't let them wake him up when I try to get him up for work either. I'm going to check her on that. She doesn't even want him to leave the house to go to work, not even to help her with the bills. She can't even buy a car because she's spending all her money on that stuff, and she has a real good job" his mom said.

"He can't be his own man. He can't ever correct himself and grow, while he's living there. Maybe she won't fight so hard if I'm not around," I said.

One morning I got a brainstorm to get some private time with Jordan. I usually rent motel rooms to take my children swimming. I took the kids to school, went to buy floats and fun toys, then went to rent the motel suite. I picked up Jordan and then the kids. The kids had so much fun swimming and we had fun watching them, but then Jordan said, "I'll be right back." Jordan didn't come back until check out time the next afternoon. He said he got caught up with his girlfriend and her druggie friends.

"I Will Always Love You" was playing on the radio when I arrived home that evening. I just sat in the car and cried to the song. After that, I gave up. It was obvious we would never be together. I started dating my high school sweetheart and first love, Bob. He had been visiting my family and had told me that he and my mom were going to make me his wife. He was also someone that I would love forever, but we had let each other go, and married other people. He was still legally married to his second wife and they had a 3-year old. The wife had left him and moved to Europe where her parents lived. She said that if he didn't move to Europe, that the marriage was over, because she would never leave her mother again. He refused to move to Europe. I think he was truly hurt about losing another wife. She was a young and pretty, half European, half African-American girl, and they had a beautiful little baby boy.

I also was still legally married, but my ex asked my permission to date my best friend back in California, and was not interested in me anymore. Nobody else approved of him dating her, but I was glad to finally see him with someone who could appreciate a nerd; even though I had to encourage him to give her the attention and affection needed to keep her, and to appreciate a good woman in reciprocation. Besides, he didn't want to leave California, and at the time, I didn't want to go back there, either. Plus, even though my mind told me to give up on Jordan and go with Bob, my heart wasn't ready to quit yet, even though I knew he wasn't trying hard enough to correct his problem.

When Jordan called, I told him that my children's father was in town to see the children. "So, that shouldn't mean that you can't come out to play with me," he said.

"Yeah, well. I'm busy and you only want to hang out on the streets anyway," I said.

"Yeah, okay. I'll holler," he said, and hung up.

Two days later he called back and said, "Yeah, I know who you're really with. We have mutual friends and I've heard the real scoop. They have even been over here telling this girl the scoop. I guess they want her to think she hasn't got to worry about you anymore," he said.

"Yeah, she doesn't," I said.

"How are you gonna get you a boyfriend?" he argued.

"What is she, chopped liver?" I asked.

He laughed and said, "Okay. I quit. Do whatever you want to do."

"You always do," I said.

I enjoyed every minute with Bob. We even went to Atlanta together for a job interview after I had gotten turned down for renting and buying a house here. That was a good thing though, because I lost my job anyway. So I planned to make my move back out of town. I had sent several resumes to the Atlanta area. I couldn't stay in a town where I couldn't even live anywhere but at my parent's house with my three kids, and where I couldn't get a permanent job. Also, if Jordan wanted to be with me, he had to be totally, completely, and permanently rehabbed, and that wasn't going to happen in this town. Anyway, he wasn't making a fast enough effort to get into rehab or out of that woman's house, so I continued planning my move and dating Bob.

Bob was very good with my children and with me, but one evening, I let him take my car to go play cards with the fellas and when he and one of the unknown players went to the gas station to buy cigarettes, the guy drove off with my car, knocking Bob down as he sped away. The police brought Bob to my house to complete the report and then took him to the hospital. Luckily, he wasn't badly hurt.

My car was a relatively new station wagon, only two years old. When they found it three days later, it was stripped of its tires and rims. Jordan was the only one with keys to it, so my dad took me to see Jordan and to get the keys. He refused to give them to me, saying I had no business letting Bob drive it. He didn't care if my Dad was sitting there in the car; he refused, unless I bought that day's supply of drugs for his habit.

I got back in the car in disbelief. I didn't want to tell my dad, and I shouldn't have, but I went on and told him that If I didn't give Jordan the $30, it would cost me $90 to have a locksmith come. My dad shook his head and said "I'm not the one he is going to disrespect like that. He's living with a woman. He shouldn't even have been driving your car, not to mention having a set of spare keys. Do what you want, but he can NEVER step foot in 'my' house again." Jordan and I made the exchange, and my dad, Bob, and I, commenced to getting my car repaired. I had no insurance. So after my dad found me some rims, Bob and I went to buy the tires. Jordan's cousin was at the tire shop that day. I had already told his family that as long as he still lived with "chopped liver" (as I called her); I was going to date whomever I wanted. Chopped Liver did have a husband though, who hung out with Jordan and me, but she was in love with Jordan. Come to think of it, she loved both of them really. She was really a nice person, just confused, and her ego confused her even more. She told me later that she was really tired of spending her money on drugs, just to keep him happy and with her.

I finally left for Atlanta after Jordan kept delaying me. He eventually checked into rehab and stayed two weeks, trying to prove to me that he really wanted to be rehabbed, but he got right back out and started taking drugs again. I would hear people whispering, "We got him with that woman so she can mess his life up on purpose. I don't know what that Erin girl is doing with him." I heard that over and over again.

I knew he had too strong of a character and was too sophisticated to get strung out on a drug like that. He was too strong to let any one woman mess up his mind. How could he be so weak to a drug that could mess up his mind? He was set up to fail, for real; probably by some of the same people who were hoping he'd get shot. A girl even put a curl in his already wavy hair, and it fell out in the top. He still looked handsome and distinguished with his new hairstyle, but I think that it was sabotage. He was so strung out, people were giving him clothes and shoes that made him look gay, and he didn't even notice, or care. They were doing that intentionally. His mom and I decided to get a lawyer to try to get him social security disability, but the lawyer gave up because he wouldn't do what she told him to do. I wrote the letters for him, but he had to show up at the hearings himself, and he wouldn't. The lawyer had no choice but to quit.

Months passed and Jordan was still calling me saying he was on the way to join me in Atlanta. He wanted to go to the Veterans' Hospital in Atlanta, far away from his drug buddies. I bought a house for me and the kids and waited some more. One day he called and asked me to drive up from Atlanta to get him, because he claimed to be "tired of being sick and sick of being tired." I happily drove up to get him, but he hadn't told the girl he lived with, anything. It was only supposed to take two days to get him out, so I only brought clothes for two days for me and the kids.

Jordan stalled for two weeks. I asked my dad to forgive Jordan for his craziness, so he and my dad had a talk.

"Sir, Erin knows I love her. I didn't have anywhere else to live, so I couldn't move out. I was just upset about her being with Bob. I apologize," Jordan said.

"I understand," my dad said, "but don't you ever disrespect me or my daughter again. I'm a man just like you are and I won't tolerate disrespect."

The next day, Jordan disappeared for 48 whole hours or so. My brother took me by Jordan's house to get my car and we saw his girlfriend leaving with her husband or somebody. It was dark and I couldn't tell for sure. My car was nowhere to be found. I asked Jordan's mom not to tell him, for fear he might try to stay around to see who she was slipping around with. When he showed up the next day he said, "My friends threw me a bachelor's party. Now I'm ready to go."

By then I didn't even have money to get back home; because I was buying food and gas for two weeks instead of two days. I had called one of my friends in Atlanta and had them get my check from my mailbox and they mailed it to me. I let Jordan know that I wasn't waiting another day, so he started easing his clothes down to my car, little by little, all day. He got most of them out when she went shopping with her friends, but he couldn't find his ID, which he needed to get into the VA hospital in Atlanta. When he quit looking for it, I just thought he was stalling again. I mysteriously found his ID on the seat of my car, but he had already gone back into her house. I gave his ID to his mom on my way to the highway back to Atlanta; and I had a car filled with his clothes. When I got home, I discovered to my surprise, that some of his girlfriend's clothes were in with his things. He had been sneaking clothes from the hamper and didn't separate them. I figured this may be my chance to get something done for him, with or without me. I washed all of their clothes, ironed them, and packed them in a box. I shipped them to her with a letter, explaining that his family and I were trying to get him off drugs, and I, Erin, did not have to be his savior. She could help him. I told her to move to the suburbs, away from the drugs, stop letting the druggies call her house, and put him back into the rehab center. I also tried to convince her to use her money to buy herself a car, instead of drugs. I knew I was stirring up some drama, but it would be worth it if it resulted in him getting clean.

"What's up?" Jordan said when he called.

"What's up with you?" I said, hoping he wasn't mad.

"She got your package," he said.

"And, is she going to help you?"

"I told her that I can't do it here, and that I had to go," he said. "She just agreed and told me to go and get my life together."

"So when are you coming," I asked.

"Girl, you are too crazy. I don't know yet," he said, trying not to sound pissed.

"My sister is gonna get me a bus ticket and get me to the bus station. I'll call you when I know the details. I was gonna ride with you," he insisted.

"Jordan, I was there two weeks, in the same clothes; and I spent all my bill money waiting for you. I have responsibilities, and children are a part of those responsibilities. If you're coming, come on. I'll be here, 'cause I'm not coming back there," I said.

I got ill while waiting and I thought I might need surgery, so I sent for my children's father to watch them until I got better. In the meantime, Bob and I had started communicating again by phone.

"Like you, Bob, if my children's father wants to help raise the kids, he has to relocate and if he doesn't, I'm filing for divorce," I said to him, hinting for him to consider filing for his divorce or to see if he was really serious enough about me, to file. But when he called me on my birthday the next week, Jordan was with me. Jordan said he always got a radar signal whenever I got ready to bring another man into the picture, so he got on the bus to Atlanta for real, after canceling with his sister twice before. Bob was really upset. He gave up on me. My children's father didn't care what I did either. After he visited around with his dad, other children, and relatives in the area, he went back to my best friend in California.

Jordan was in and out of rehab four times in two months. As soon as he would get out, he would go straight to the liquor store and elsewhere. People were saying, "He won't be here long. A change of environment is not going to help him." It sounded, again, like that was a plan. The VA even delayed his entrance for a couple of weeks, and they didn't successfully rehab him. People were saying all kinds of negative things about him; especially people who were worse than he. "He was always a dope addict. He's a thug. He beats women. He's never had his own place or his own car."

Yet I remember back in his hey day when all the men wanted to live where he lived; have the quality ladies he had, ride in his or Rick's cars. I even remember when I heard some of the jealous guys say, "They were square genius-like intellectuals in high school. How did they get so popular with all the ladies, all of a sudden?" Now nobody said anything good about him or his brother, except that his body must be made of solid gold for me to stick with him. Therefore not many people were willing to help me, **really help him**; plus he was a bit hard headed with me and his mom. So, I had to send him back home. I finally realized that I couldn't help him. I didn't know rehab was so hard.

I thought all I had to do was change his environment and put him in a program; but there was a wagon, and he kept falling off that wagon. It was nerve-wrecking and the rehab place turned out impossible results. I kept in touch, trying to keep him thinking in terms of rehab. He did keep checking himself in and out, over a dozen times. I got back into writing songs, acting, and business adventures. He hung out with me and the kids in my hotel room when I returned home for a business expo and convention.

He and the kids went to the pizza parlor, got room service food, and had fun together. I eventually did move back home and was working everyday, but he wasn't rehabbed or driving.

"My mind is so messed up. I don't even think I can pass the written driving test," he said.

"You should at least try," I told him.

"They'll let you take it over and over, until you pass," I pleaded, to no avail. I finally gave up. I stopped calling. I stopped driving him around everywhere, for it seemed that we were driving around in circles. He also finally accepted that he had lost his chance at a happy life with me. I am now remarried and have gotten my doctorate degree in business.

I kept the songs that I had written. I plan to give them to my children who also have musical talents. I hope my directions will lead my children into singing. I have also published a couple of books and I have written and acted in a couple of movies. I won't do anything foolish to mess up my life or my children's life. Therefore, life with an addict, on and off the wagon, and the money problems that go with that life are something with which I will NEVER again have dealings. Yet, STILL in the back of my mind I hated to see people intentionally mess up Jordan's life. So for one last time, I called to check on him.

"Rick. It's me, Erin, Jordan's unofficial wife."

"Oh, hi baby. How have you been?"

"I've been fine. How are you? And, how is he?"

"I'm fine. Him -- same o, same o."

"If I can get him in the best rehab that I know of, do you think you can convince him to check himself in?"

"I'm not sure. If tell him it's your idea, he might go."

"Yeah, but I don't want him to think
that I'm reuniting with him, and I will never send him anything to enable his habit. You guys will have to find him a new place to reside before he gets out, and set him up in some sort of business.

I'm not sure that paralegal thing is a good idea. He'll again be around the same kind of people that keep him in trouble. You think you can create him a job and an income?" I asked.

"That's a possibility," Rick said, thinking.

"Also, check on his son and get him
permanently on the straight and narrow too. We can't let anything happen to any of these kids; and we can't let them follow in any misdirected footsteps. We have to save them too. I'll call you back when I have him registered in a rehab. If you need his son registered in the rehab too, call me back and let me know. My number is on your caller ID, isn't it?"

"Yes. I'll take care of it," Rick answered. "Where is he going?"

"Not sure yet. Texas, Alabama, Jersey, maybe even Betty Ford. I've got to double check my sources. Don't worry about transportation; I'll take care of that too. I'll call you back tomorrow, if not tonight. Love you," I said.

"Love you too, baby," he said.

Two years later, Rick called me on my cell phone. "I heard you were going to be touring near here. Why don't you meet me? I want you to see your finished project."

I met Rick, who is now a pastor, at the pastor's house on the grounds behind the church. We went into the backdoor up to the loft. Looking down into a closed-in section of the church we saw Jordan holding a brand new baby girl. A beautiful woman was sitting next to him. He was reading from the Bible to a room full of parishioners, explaining what each passage meant.

"He's my deacon now, and that's his new wife and baby. He's also going to school to become a full-fledged minister. I built two other houses on the property, one for him and one for his son. His son is a deacon too and the director of youth activities, praise dancing, directing the youth choir, and the youth Bible study. I thank you so much," he said as he hugged me, "and my mom thanks you, too. He turned out to be a 'Sweet Scorpion' after all."

The End

Ami

Ami

www.ingramcontent.com/pod-product-compliance
Lightning Source LLC
Chambersburg PA
CBHW060823120626
46557CB00001B/348